WOODROW WILSON
PRESIDENT

Other Books in the Presidential Biography Series

JIMMY CARTER, PRESIDENT
Betsy Covington Smith

DWIGHT DAVID EISENHOWER, PRESIDENT
Elizabeth Van Steenwyk

GERALD R. FORD, PRESIDENT
Sallie G. Randolph

LYNDON BAINES JOHNSON, PRESIDENT
John Devaney

RICHARD M. NIXON, PRESIDENT
Sallie G. Randolph

RONALD REAGAN, PRESIDENT
John Devaney

FRANKLIN DELANO ROOSEVELT, PRESIDENT
John Devaney

**FIVE FIRST LADIES: A Look into the Lives of
Nancy Reagan, Rosalynn Carter, Betty Ford, Pat
Nixon, and Lady Bird Johnson**
Elizabeth Simpson Smith

WOODROW WILSON PRESIDENT

Sallie G. Randolph

Walker and Company
New York

First published in the United States of America in 1992
by Walker Publishing Company, Inc.

Published simultaneously in Canada by Thomas Allen & Son
Canada, Limited, Markham, Ontario

Library of Congress Cataloging-in-Publication Data
Randolph, Sallie G.
    Woodrow Wilson, president / Sallie G. Randolph.
        p. cm.
    Includes index.
    Summary: Discusses the life of the American president who decided
to enter World War I despite his quest for peace.
    ISBN 0-8027-8143-8. —ISBN 0-8027-8144-6 (lib. bdg.)
    1. Wilson, Woodrow, 1856–1924—Juvenile literature.
2. Presidents—United States—Biography—Juvenile literature.
3. United States—Politics and government—1913–1921—Juvenile
literature. [1. Wilson, Woodrow, 1856–1924. 2. Presidents.]
I. Title.
E767.R27   1992
973.91'3'092—dc20
[B]   91-23589
                                                               CIP
                                                                AC

Printed in the United States of America

10 9 8 7 6 5 4 3 2 1

For three special women:
Kate Ennis Mabbette,
Geneva Maude Ennis,
and in loving memory of
Lewise Ennis Beutler.

CONTENTS

Acknowledgments

It wouldn't have been possible to write this book without the help of others, particularly the dedicated librarians and staff of the Buffalo and Erie County Public Library, the Town of Concord Public Library, the Crane Library, the Elma Public Library, the Kenmore Public Library, the St. Louis Public Library, the Library of Congress, and the National Archives of the United States. Others who provided generous assistance include Kate Ennis Mabbette, Robert O. Wieland, Alice E. Glazier, Will Randolph, Kathy Campbell, Dr. and Mrs. Ralph W. Loew, Katherine G. Sathi, Ned Cuddy, Suzanne Bissonette, Erin Harrington, and John Randolph. Amy Shields and Jeanne Gardner, fine editors and producers of high-quality books for young readers, also deserve special thanks.

WOODROW WILSON
PRESIDENT

1

The Bitter Brink of War

Woodrow Wilson, president of the United States of America, sat alone in his White House office, his lean face gaunt with fatigue. He studied his typewritten notes and went over his options once again. His head throbbed, the pain radiating from his temples down his neck, a pain that had plagued him from childhood in times of stress. It was late on Sunday evening, Palm Sunday and April Fools' Day in 1917. The cold drizzle outside matched his somber mood.

Midnight came. The first hour of Monday, April 2, ticked by. The misty streets of Washington were mostly deserted, except for the cab that pulled up under the White House portico and discharged a solitary passenger. The visitor, a trusted friend and newspaper editor, was shown into Wilson's office. The president looked up, his features stretched by tension into a near caricature of himself. He described to his friend the sleepless nights he had endured, the repeated disappointment he had faced, the agony he had suffered during his long struggle to remain neutral in the war that raged in Europe, and his growing realization that entering that distant war was inevitable. "I have never been so unsure of anything in my life before," he said.

The editor tried to offer words of solace. The president's hand had been forced by the actions of the Germans, he said. If the nation was going to war, it certainly wasn't Wilson's fault. Hadn't he worked tirelessly for peace? Wilson had done all that it was humanly possible to do. He had pushed himself almost beyond the limits of his endurance. America's entrance into the war simply couldn't be helped.

The weary president shook his head, the naturally prim expression on his long face deepened by the crisis, light glinting off the lenses of his rimless spectacles. America was taking a sad and inevitable step. "Once lead this people into war and they'll forget there ever was such a thing as tolerance. To fight you must be brutal and ruthless," he said. "The spirit of ruthless brutality will enter into the very fiber of our national life, infecting Congress, the courts, the policeman on the beat, the man in the street." He shuddered at the forces of hatred that he would soon unleash.

He told his companion that war would overturn the world they had known. "It would mean that we should lose our heads along with the rest and stop weighing right and wrong. It would mean that a majority of people in this hemisphere would go war-mad, quit thinking, and devote their energies to destruction." The Constitution, he feared, was threatened. Free speech and the right of assembly might not survive. Legal and moral restraints would loosen, industry would become greedy and amoral, profiteering would run rampant. War would bring ghastly changes. "If there is any alternative, for God's sake, let's take it," he cried.

Dawn came, but no alternative presented itself. The drizzle continued. "Momentous day," Edith Wilson, the president's wife, wrote that morning in her diary.

Woodrow Wilson was serving his second term of office, having been reelected in 1916 after a campaign based on the slogan "He kept us out of war." Now he was preparing to enter the very war he had struggled so hard to avoid. All his efforts to negotiate an end to the conflict that consumed the nations of Europe had failed, and the determination of the United States to remain neutral had been threatened by Germany's increasing acts of hostility.

The American public had been clamoring for war. The voices

of the hawks in Congress were becoming increasingly strident. Wilson's close advisers were pressing the president to wage war on Germany. War fever was mounting, but Wilson had resisted taking the ultimate step.

"We are not governed by public opinion," he had said at a cabinet meeting two weeks before. "I want to be right whether it is popular or not." But the belligerent activities of Germany grew harder and harder to ignore. Neutrality became ever more difficult for America to maintain. The pressure grew. The president reviewed his options. "What else can I do?" he asked an adviser. The difficult answer was now clear.

It was very early when Edith Wilson found the president brooding on the South Portico. She brought him some milk and biscuits and draped an overcoat across his shoulders. An adviser had said to him that he was "too refined, too civilized, too intellectual, too cultivated" for war, Wilson told his wife. The adviser had been right, he said. Although he wanted to learn from the mistakes of Madison, Lincoln, and the others who had held office before him, he was afraid, terribly afraid that he wouldn't do well at making war.

As people geared up for the new April day, talk of war dominated conversations all over the country. Pacifists, those who believed that the United States should stay out of the war, argued with "hawks," who thought that America's rightful place was aligned against Germany, alongside Great Britain and its allies.

Activists for many causes—peace, war, the vote for women, labor rights, patriotism, and a variety of others—were in Washington that day. As the day went on, officials feared disruption. One avid hawk, in fact, Senator Henry Cabot Lodge, a longtime adversary of President Wilson, was insulted by a pacifist in a hallway of the Capitol. The crusty old senator responded by lashing out with a surprisingly effective punch.

It was the opening day of Congress, and the president had asked to address a joint session of the Senate and House of

President Woodrow Wilson asks a joint session of Congress for a declaration of war on April 2, 1917. (National Archives)

Representatives. Routine organizing had to take place first, so the president waited for notification that Congress was assembled to hear him. "Congress convened at 12 noon; called in special session to declare war," Edith Wilson wrote in her diary. "The House did not organize in time for the Message to be delivered until 8:30 p.m."

The hours dragged by for the beleaguered president. Mrs. Wilson, who considered daily exercise vital to her husband's health, sent him off to play a round of golf, hoping some fresh air would help him relax. He went over his notes yet again, discussing his speech with the secretary of state and another close adviser. He had a light lunch, although his digestion, always delicate, was rebelling against the tension.

Visitors to the White House and inquiries from the press were turned away as the long afternoon passed and the presidential party waited for word from Congress. The secretary of state feared danger from the growing crowds, among whom there had been several outbreaks of violence, and urged that the president ride to the Capitol under armed guard. Wilson refused, although a ceremonial cavalry escort was arranged.

The president went to the State, War, and Navy Building to hold brief meetings with the secretary of war and top military leaders. He returned to the White House for a quick dinner with his family and advisers before setting out to make his historic speech.

The president's huge motor limousine was escorted from the White House to the Capitol by soldiers on horseback. The presidential party passed thousands of people who waved flags and cheered. A cold spring rain fell, giving the lighted streets the look of an Impressionist painting. Ahead, the dome of the Capitol was bathed in dramatic lights.

"When we reached the Capitol the crowd outside was almost as dense as Inauguration Day, but perfectly orderly," Edith Wilson wrote. "Troops were standing on guard round the entire building which stood out white and majestic in the indirect lighting which was used for the first time this eventful night."

At the Capitol, the president went to a private room reserved for his use. He needed a few moments to compose himself. He walked to the mirror and stared hard at his image. His face was contorted with distress, his features so twisted that the side of his mouth drooped. Drawing on inner resources, he pulled his body up straight. He smoothed the planes of his face into stern regularity with one hand, forcing his features back into rigid symmetry. He pushed his jaw into line with the other hand.

"Gentlemen, the president of the United States," the Speaker of the House intoned.

Woodrow Wilson stepped into the vast chamber, which was filled with members of both houses of Congress, almost every one carrying or wearing a small American flag. The room was also crowded with members of the cabinet, military officers, Supreme Court justices, and other important government leaders. The entire diplomatic corps, with the exception of the German delegation, which had been asked to leave the country a month before, had been invited to hear the president's speech. These representatives of foreign governments, many dressed in full native regalia, added an element of color to the glitter of braid and the glint of brass.

Correspondents jammed the press gallery, and the visitors' gallery was packed with important guests. The president's wife, his daughter Margaret, his cousin, his personal secretary, and a close adviser occupied the front row.

The gathering was quiet, though, and expectant. "I could hear people breathing, so still was this great throng," Edith Wilson wrote. "When my husband came in and all rose to their feet my very heart seemed to stop its beating."

As the president approached the rostrum, an ovation broke out and grew into a great wave of cheers and applause that lasted for more than two minutes. It was the most applause this president had ever received in Congress, but Wilson didn't smile or acknowledge it except with a slight, grave bow. He took out his notes and placed them on the lectern. The chamber grew silent except for an occasional cough and the patter of rain on the dome above. The president's hands trembled, the only visible sign of his distress. His voice was low and steady.

"I have called the Congress into extraordinary session because there are serious, very serious, choices of policy to be made, and made immediately," he told the nation's assembled leadership. The momentous decision was not constitutionally his, he added, then he outlined the series of recent events that had made such a decision necessary. His voice seemed to swell as he continued. "With a profound sense of the solemn and even tragical character of the step I am taking and of the grave responsibilities which it involves, but in unhesitating obedience to what I deem my constitutional duty, I advise that the

Congress declare the recent course of the Imperial German Government to be in fact nothing less than war against the government and people of the United States."

He stood straight, his face still stern. His hands no longer trembled as he continued to explain, in clear, straightforward terms, exactly why he was asking for a declaration of war. "The world must be made safe for democracy," he said. "Its peace must be planted upon the tested foundation of political liberty. We have no selfish ends to serve. We desire no conquest, no dominion. We seek no indemnities for ourselves, no material compensation for the sacrifices we shall freely make."

The compelling speech continued for almost half an hour. The audience listened in respectful silence as the president explained that this war would not be waged for America's gain but in order to create peace. He outlined the conflict as a great battle between the forces of good and evil. "We are but one of the champions of the rights of mankind. We shall be satisfied when those rights have been made as secure as the faith and the freedom of nations can make them," he said. "The day has come when America is privileged to spend her blood and her might for the principles that gave her birth and happiness and the peace which she has treasured. God helping her, she can do no other."

The great room was momentarily silent, breathlessly so. Some cried openly. Some hugged. Then came a spate of vigorous clapping and a few cheers. People rose to their feet. The clapping grew into a wave of applause that vibrated throughout the chamber. The cheering swelled in crescendo.

The president stepped down from the podium and walked through the chamber. His political archenemy, Senator Lodge, stopped him on the way out. "Mr. President," he said, "you have expressed in the loftiest manner possible the sentiments of the American people."

Correspondents dashed from the press gallery to call their newspapers. Word spread quickly to the growing crowds outside. The president's war message was telegraphed around the world. The news was announced to hearty applause and emotional demonstrations of patriotism at theaters, concert halls, and other public gatherings in Washington, New York, and cities and towns across America. It was greeted with joy in Britain and France and with anxious belligerence in Germany.

The president left the Capitol. Swell after swell of loud cheering followed his limousine down Pennsylvania Avenue, the frenetic crowds undiscouraged by the cold rain. Damp flags and soggy bunting hung limp in the background, in sharp contrast to the mood of the people, who expressed their enthusiasm with shouts, applause, and waving of their flags and banners.

The president didn't acknowledge the throngs who lined the route back to the White House, except for a sad remark to his secretary. "Think what it was they were applauding. My message today was a message of death to our young men. How strange that they should applaud." He shook his head again and observed that life in America, "until this thing is over, and God only knows when it will be over, will be full of tragedy and heartaches."

Later the president, drained and exhausted, sat in the Cabinet Room at the White House with his personal secretary. "I shall never forget that scene," the secretary later wrote. The president "appeared like a man who had thrown off old burdens only to add new ones."

The two men discussed the impending war, the events leading up to it, the terrible burdens of leadership that had been imposed on Wilson, and the trials yet to come. As they talked, the emotional impact of the past weeks caught up with the president, who, according to the secretary's account, "drew his handkerchief from his pocket, wiped away great tears that stood in his eyes, and then, laying his head on the Cabinet table, sobbed as if he had been a child."

2

Peaceful Childhood

It was just a few minutes before midnight on December 28, 1856, when Thomas Woodrow Wilson was born in a big downstairs room of the imposing brick manse, home of the minister of the First Presbyterian Church in Staunton, Virginia. Tommy was the first son of the Reverend Doctor Joseph Ruggles Wilson and Janet Woodrow Wilson. The Wilsons, already the parents of two daughters, were delighted that their third child was a boy, and they named the new baby after his maternal grandfather, Thomas Woodrow, also a Presbyterian minister.

"He is a fine healthy fellow," his mother, whom everyone called Jessie, soon told her friends, neighbors, and family. "He is as little trouble as it is possible for a baby to be."

Later that night, Joseph Wilson climbed the stairs to his second-floor study. "Thomas Woodrow Wilson was born at 12¾ o'clock," he penned in his distinctive handwriting in the big family Bible. After recording the birth, he offered a long prayer of thanksgiving and hope for his new baby boy.

"You may be sure Joseph is very proud of his fine little son," Jessie Wilson wrote in a letter, "though he used to say daughters were so much sweeter than sons."

"That baby is dignified enough to be moderator of the General Assembly," a relative said the first time he saw Thomas Woodrow Wilson. He may have looked dignified enough, even as a baby, to be a politician, but his parents were sure their son would grow up to be a Presbyterian minister, just like his father and grandfather.

The Presbyterian manse in Staunton, Virginia, where Thomas Woodrow Wilson was born on December 28, 1856. (The Library of Congress)

Joseph Ruggles Wilson would be the dominant influence in his son's life, helping to shape the boy into the strong personality who would emerge. He was an impressive figure of a man—intelligent, determined, educated, handsome, and somewhat egotistical. He was deeply religious, although his staunch Presbyterian views were tempered by small indulgences such as an occasional drink and a good pipe. He could be stern, demanding, and unyielding, although he was also known for a lively sense of humor and his enjoyment of a good romp.

Janet Woodrow Wilson was more reserved than her husband. A gifted singer and pianist, she passed on to her son a fine voice along with her clear gray eyes and plain, even features.

When Thomas Wilson was still a baby, his family moved from Virginia to the thriving Deep South town of Augusta, Georgia,

A corner in the parlor of the Presbyterian manse in Staunton, Virginia, furnished as it probably was at the time of the future president's birth. (National Archives)

where Joseph Wilson became pastor of the First Presbyterian Church. Tommy spent the next dozen years of his boyhood in this prosperous, pleasant community. The family's home was a spacious brick manse shaded by stately trees. Here Tommy was nurtured by a warm family life and shaped by his exposure to great events of the times.

The baby who was "just as good as he could be" continued to be very little trouble as he grew into a boy in the close-knit Wilson family. He was doted on by his mother, taught and challenged by his father, and indulged by his two older sisters, Marion and Anne.

From his very early childhood on, Tommy Wilson loved to listen and learn. Experience and discussion made an indelible impression on him, and experiences became meaningful to him because he mixed them with discussion and analysis. He asked lots of questions, and he thought about things. He had a rich fantasy life and invented elaborate games to play when he was alone.

Religion played an important role in his life. "When he was so small that his feet barely touched the floor and too young to understand the sermon, Tommy was so fascinated by his father's beautiful voice and resounding phrases that he was only occasionally conscious of his thin frame growing numb on the uncushioned pew," wrote one of his daughters. "There were also the hymns—the fine, stern Presbyterian hymns. He knew them all by heart and he had a good ear for music and raised his voice lustily with the rest of the congregation."

Tommy loved his mother, who gave him uncritical love and confidence in his own considerable abilities. Some people even called him a mama's boy and felt he might be too dependent on his mother. Others said that you can't spoil a child with too much love and that Tommy's relationship with his mother allowed him to grow into an emotionally healthy adult in spite of physical problems and some early difficulties in learning to read.

Even as a very young boy, Tommy was a dreamer and a thinker whose distinguished father was the most important person in the world to him—teacher, mentor, hero, and friend. The Rev. Dr. Joseph Wilson thought of the mind not as a "gut to be stuffed" but as a "digestive" and "assimilating" organ. Tommy's natural inclination to digest and assimilate the experiences of his life was encouraged by the man he called an "incomparable father."

One such experience was Tommy's earliest awareness of war. "My first recollection is of standing at my father's gateway in Augusta, Georgia, when I was four years old, and hearing someone pass and say that Mr. Lincoln was elected and there was to be war. Catching the intense tones of his excited voice, I remember running in to ask my father what it meant."

What it meant was the coming of the Civil War. Although the worst ravages of that war would spare Augusta, Tommy's experiences and observations of it during the formative years of his boyhood would shape his thinking as an adult and eventually have a lasting impact on the course of history. It was his childhood struggle to understand war that taught Tommy Wilson the value of peace.

Although there wasn't actual fighting in Augusta, the Presbyterian church was turned into a hospital, where Tommy saw the suffering of wounded soldiers and heard terrible accounts of the battles and their horrors. Prisoners of war, feared Yankee soldiers, were briefly incarcerated in the churchyard. There were wartime shortages to deal with and, for a while, fear that General Sherman's fearful march to the sea would go through Augusta.

The war also disrupted education, and Tommy Wilson didn't attend school or learn to read until after he was nine years old. But that didn't mean he didn't receive an excellent, if unorthodox, education, with his father as teacher. Dr. Wilson took him on regular expeditions to factories and mills, stores and banks, where Tommy learned firsthand how things work and how people function in a society. Those visits and long talks with his father afterward taught Tommy more than he could learn in any school. Years later he would describe the "gigantic engines, the roar of furnaces, or the darting up of sheets of flame, the great forges presided over by imps with sooty faces," as his most valuable educational experience.

Dr. Wilson urged his son to think, choose, revise, and debate. "Steady now, Thomas," he would say. "Wait a minute. Think. Think what it is you wish to say and then choose your words to say it."

Even though he didn't read, Tommy enjoyed being read to and absorbed information and ideas from listening. Reading aloud was an important family activity in the Wilson household. The Bible, of course, was common fare. But the novels of Charles Dickens and Sir Walter Scott were popular too.

After the war was over, Tommy attended a school that had been established by a returning Confederate soldier, but he didn't do very well. He was bored by the drill that he and the other students were expected to do. He complained that there was too much "stuffing" of his mind at school and not enough assimilating and digesting. He also had a lot of trouble learning to read.

Until he started school, there had been no need for him to read because his mother and father both read to him. His parents had tried to teach him the alphabet and how to sound out words, but Tommy wasn't responsive. His eyesight was poor, so his parents didn't push and Tommy was content to learn by listening.

Modern experts now think that Tommy Wilson had a learning disability called dyslexia, which caused him to see some words and letters backward and made both writing and reading difficult skills to master. It was especially lucky that his education was delayed and that his parents read to him so extensively, because that is the way educators of today think dyslexic students should be taught.

A view of the Wilson birthplace from the street side. The building has been restored and is now a museum open to the public. (The Library of Congress)

Tommy's willingness to read on his own may have been expedited by the birth of his younger brother, Joseph Ruggles Wilson, Jr., called Josie, who came along when Tommy was ten years old. Now that his mother and sisters didn't have long hours to read to him and now that his growing curiosity needed more and more feeding, Tommy became an avid reader. Once the habit took hold, it became a lifelong passion, and he was almost never without a book.

Along with reading came an interest in writing. As Tommy struggled to write, he often brought his efforts to his father, who would challenge him to polish them. "When you frame a sentence," his father told him, "don't do it as if you're loading a shotgun, but as if you're loading a rifle. Shoot with a single bullet and hit one thing alone." Another time Dr. Wilson urged him to "make your mind like a needle, of one eye and a single point."

Oratory also fascinated Tommy. As the son of a minister, he was exposed to the power of the spoken word and the well-delivered speech. Before he was even capable of understanding their meaning, he was entranced by the flow and cadence of sermons. As he grew up, he used to practice speaking in the empty church. He'd climb to the pulpit and look out over the rows of pews, imagining an audience assembled to hear his words. Sometimes he would deliver famous speeches from the past. Other times he would put his own ideas into words, struggling to find the best phrases and the right gestures.

Tommy had other interests too. He and his friends formed a combination baseball team and debating society that they called the Lightfoot Club. Because the club met in his father's hayloft, Tommy was elected president. He took his duties seriously and conducted meetings according to strict parliamentary procedure. He also wrote a constitution for the club.

"Light Foot Base Ball Club, Thomas Woodrow Wilson, Augusta Georgia, 1870," he penciled in elaborately painstaking block letters on the inside cover of a schoolbook, *Elements of Physical Geography.* The drawing included a roster of nine club members and detailed sketches of two hot-air balloons, one topped by a Confederate flag. "T. W. Wilson . . . 2nd Base" was the fourth name on the list of members.

When Tommy was nearly fourteen, his family moved to Columbia, South Carolina, where Dr. Wilson became professor at a Presbyterian seminary. Columbia, the state capital, had been in the path of General Sherman and had been devastated by war. The young teenager was shocked by the poverty, desolation, and exploitation in its aftermath, and his abhorrence of war was reinforced.

In Columbia, Tommy attended a small private school. He didn't much like it, and he didn't do particularly well at Latin and Greek, but he did a lot of reading on his own. His favorite books were adventure stories, and he often imagined himself as the hero of various adventures, particularly swashbuckling ones on the high seas.

During this period in his life, Tommy Wilson discovered a method of speed writing called shorthand and taught himself to use it. He also taught himself to type and began to write papers and letters on a portable typewriter. After that he made extensive reading notes in shorthand and began to write prolifically. These were fortunate discoveries, because the physical act of writing is very difficult for learning-disabled students to master. Shorthand and typing took the frustration out of writing and helped make Wilson's later academic success possible.

Besides his school studies and reading, young Thomas Wilson attended his father's church regularly and listened avidly to Dr. Wilson's sermons, which the local newspaper called "uniformly able and interesting—full of fresh and vigorous thought."

Because his father also taught at the seminary, Tommy spent a lot of time sitting in classes there, listening with interest to the debates among the professors and the discussions of the students. His favorite professor, of course, was his father, whose skill with words and speech Tommy longed to emulate. He used to play a game with himself. Whenever his father paused during a lecture or sermon, Tommy would try to come up with the next word before his father did. "Sometimes I would try swiftly in my own mind to supply it," he later wrote, "but rarely found the inevitable word as he did."

An older seminary student, who was studying for the ministry and planned to be a crusading evangelist, began holding small revival services, which Tommy attended. During the summer of 1873, Tommy experienced a gradual spiritual awakening and decided, to the delight of his parents, to ask for formal membership in the Presbyterian Church. From that time on,

Thomas Woodrow Wilson's deep and abiding faith remained with him, the foundation of a bedrock idealism and absolute confidence that would shape the emerging man.

When he was seventeen years old, Tommy's family sent him away to Davidson College, a small Presbyterian school in North Carolina where they hoped he would begin studying for the ministry. He was terribly homesick there, and painfully shy, although he joined the debating club, where his practice and ability served him well. He even wrote a new constitution for the organization.

The studies at Davidson were difficult for him, partly because he had to learn what his teachers wanted him to, whereas before he had been generally free to read and study whatever interested him, and partly because his grounding in basic academic subjects was not very strong. He resented the restrictions formal study imposed on the time he spent in reading, dreaming, and recreation.

Getting away from home was a valuable experience for Tommy in many ways. His family life was nurturing, but it could be stifling too. At Davidson, Tommy became more independent, although he was also miserable and ill much of the time. In the spring he suffered through a series of colds that deepened into chest complaints and spasms of serious coughing. The stress and unhappiness of being away from home undoubtedly aggravated his condition, so that by the time he returned to Columbia in June he was close to a physical breakdown.

He begged not to go back to Davidson in the fall and stayed home the next year, studying on his own, attending church, sitting in on lectures at the seminary, and perfecting his ability with the Graham method of shorthand. In 1874 the family moved again, this time so Dr. Wilson could become the pastor of a large church in the seaport town of Wilmington, North Carolina.

Tommy, now a daydreaming young man of eighteen, was fascinated by the docks and spent hours poking around among

Tommy Wilson (middle row, third from right, holding his hat) was a member of the Alligator Club at Princeton. The Alligator Club was one of several eating clubs, similar to fraternities, where students dined and socialized. (The Library of Congress)

the ships that came and went. He found these forays far more appealing than the tutoring in Greek and other formal subjects that he was receiving from an Episcopal clergyman and the growing pressure from his father to buckle down to his studies so he could continue his preparation to enter the ministry. His religious faith was as strong as ever, but he had doubts about becoming a minister.

The idea of sailing across the ocean to the types of adventures he had dreamed about for so long was so much more enticing, in fact, that he actually decided to go to sea. He talked to a friendly ship's captain and was ready to sign on as a crew member. But when he told his mother about his plans, she talked him out of them. Soon his parents decided it was time for Tommy to resume his formal education, this time at Princeton College in New Jersey, where his father had earned a degree.

Tommy was tall, skinny, and almost nineteen when he arrived at Princeton as a freshman. He struggled through his first year, finding the work more difficult and challenging than any he had faced before. His second year, though, was a turning point. The work became easier and more interesting. He found himself reading all the time and was especially fascinated by politics, government, and history. He was active in debating and skilled in writing; he won a prize for an essay on one European statesman and had an article about another published. He began to consider a career in politics and often daydreamed about being elected governor or senator. He even bought a packet of blank calling cards and entertained himself by inscribing them "Thomas Woodrow Wilson, Senator from Virginia."

Tommy Wilson thrived in the stimulating and tranquil atmosphere of the Princeton campus and by the time he graduated in 1879 had amassed an impressive record with awards, recognition, reasonably good grades, and popularity. He had finally conquered his shyness and was more self-confident than ever before. A significant achievement, unusual for an undergraduate student, was the publication of his essay "Cabinet Government in the United States" in a prestigious national magazine, the *International Review*. The editor who accepted Wilson's essay was Henry Cabot Lodge, who would one day become a powerful senator and a bitter rival.

3

Scholar and Teacher

After he graduated from Princeton in June of 1879, Tommy Wilson went home to the manse in Wilmington to rest and enjoy a recuperative summer with his family. He vacationed with his mother, his sister Anne and her three children, and his younger brother in the Blue Ridge Mountains. He corresponded extensively with his childhood and college friends. He did a lot of reading and writing. He broke the news to his disappointed father that he did not intend to become a minister. He was fascinated by government and more interested in a career in politics, so he decided to study law.

In the fall he traveled to Charlottesville, Virginia, to attend law school at the University of Virginia. On the beautiful campus of the great university, which had been founded by Thomas Jefferson, he studied under some great teachers, but he found himself mired in the detail and technicalities that his law courses focused on when his real interest was the impact of law on society, politics, and history. "I am most terribly bored by the noble study of Law sometimes," he wrote to a friend, "though I am thoroughly satisfied with my choice of profession." The problem was a lack of variety, stifling to a student who had always been encouraged to indulge in wide-ranging intellectual discussion, reading, and investigations. "This excellent thing, the Law, gets as monotonous as that other immortal article of food, Hash, when served with such endless frequency," he wrote.

As his first year of law school progressed, Thomas Wilson's

old health problems recurred. Chronic indigestion plagued him. He suffered from headaches and "dyspepsia." His illness was probably caused, at least in part, by stress and worry. His family urged him to come home for a rest, but Wilson struggled through the year.

After a summer of rest, he felt better and returned to Charlottesville in the fall. But the resumption of his studies brought a further decline in his health. In December he decided to leave school and returned to his family abruptly. In those days it wasn't necessary to attend law school in order to become a lawyer. Wilson continued to study on his own for the next year and a half.

By the summer of 1882, Wilson was twenty-five years old, a tall, lean young man with a prim, dignified look. When he smiled, though, and a sparkle came into his clear gray eyes, he was almost handsome. He had rested, studied, and recuperated reasonably well from the indigestion and illness that had flared up so often during stressful times. He had also decided to drop his first name and now called himself Woodrow Wilson. It was time to get on with his life and pursue his dream of a political career.

He had studied law because he believed it to be the way to achieve his goal of winning political office. He and a friend from law school, Edward I. Renick, decided to start a legal practice together. They picked Atlanta, the booming new center of the postwar South, as a place with lots of opportunity. Atlanta, big, raw, and vital, did offer plenty of opportunity to the aggressive and ambitious, but neither Wilson nor Renick, both sheltered and scholarly, was the type to thrive in such an atmosphere.

They rented a small office on the second floor of a commercial building at 48 Marietta Street in downtown Atlanta and proudly put up a sign, "Renick and Wilson." They let rooms from a widow on nearby Peachtree Street. Woodrow began to attend the Presbyterian church and even met an attractive young woman with whom he went for Sunday afternoon walks. In October he took and passed his bar examination with flying colors. His friendship with Renick grew as the two young attorneys discovered how well they complemented each other and how alike they were. They passed many hours in stimulating discussion. They read books, shared ideas, and debated the issues of the day. But they didn't practice much law.

While Woodrow was right that working as a lawyer was the usual route to political success, he hadn't counted on the fact that the process was a slow one, and he wasn't interested enough in the nuts and bolts of legal work to endure the years of tedious drudgery it would take to reach his goal. He had also assumed, naively, that the role of lawyers was to serve the good of society, and he was genuinely shocked by nature of the work. Instead of serving lofty ideals, lawyers, he discovered, were expected to get scoundrels and crooks off the hook without paying the price for their misdeeds, help sleazy business owners squirm out of their moral responsibilities, represent narrow-minded clients in petty squabbles, or slog through mires of boring detail to settle routine legal matters. Even worse, Atlanta was overflowing with young lawyers, and the competition for such degrading work was brutal.

"Here the chief end of man is certainly to make money, and money cannot be made except by the most vulgar methods," Woodrow wrote. "The studious man is pronounced impractical and is suspected as a visionary." There was a big difference, he had found, between the dream and the reality. "The philosophical study of the law, which must be a pleasure to any thoughtful man, is a very different matter from its scheming and haggling practice."

The strategy of the two young lawyers was to take the high road and accept only honorable cases. Eventually, they hoped, they would build a reputation. In the meantime, they continued their richly enjoyable intellectual pursuits. Woodrow's only client for legal services was his mother, who asked him to manage her modest business affairs. He had no outlet for his oratorical skills either, other than a brief opportunity to speak before a tariff commission that held hearings in Atlanta. He studied the issues and made a stirring speech against protective tariffs, but the bored commissioners, for whom the hearing was a mere formality, were "ill natured and sneering," and there was no interested audience to be swayed by the force of his oratory and give him the enthusiastic feedback that was so necessary.

Perhaps their strategy would have worked if Woodrow and his partner had been willing to give it enough time. But Woodrow had to borrow money from his father to pay his bills, and after six months in Atlanta he was thoroughly disillusioned. By the spring of 1883, he realized that his choice of a career had been a mistake and he began to reconsider his options.

After less than a year in Atlanta, he decided to abandon the law along with his hopes of political office and retreat to the academic and intellectual world, which was more conducive to his nature. Although it was agonizing and he regretted giving up his chance in politics, a burden was lifted once he had made this decision.

Woodrow feared that he might be a malcontent who would drift from one job to another, one career to the next. But he already knew that he had a good mind, that he loved to study, write, and speak, and that he had a passion for the subject of politics. Maybe he could find a place for himself as a college professor. He learned of a graduate school, Johns Hopkins University in Baltimore, Maryland, that had started to offer a suitable course of study, and he decided to apply.

"A professorship was the only feasible place for me," he wrote, "the only place that would afford leisure for reading and for original work, the only strictly literary berth with an income attached." The only drawback, from his point of view, was that he wouldn't be able to "participate actively in public affairs" but would have to content himself "with becoming an outside force in politics."

One good thing resulted from Woodrow Wilson's brief and unsuccessful career as a lawyer. When he traveled to Rome, Georgia, on legal business for his mother, he attended the

Presbyterian church and noticed a young woman with a "bright, pretty face" and "splendid, laughing eyes" who turned out to be the minister's daughter.

At first he thought that the captivating girl must be married. She sat with a young boy, who Woodrow decided must be her son. Then he noticed that she wore a heavy crepe veil, a sign of mourning. A widow, then, he thought. Angrily, he rebuked himself for being jealous of a man he had never met and tried to concentrate on the sermon. Normally he had tremendous powers of concentration, but they failed him now. His eyes and thoughts kept drifting back to the pretty woman in black. After the service he asked his aunt about her and learned, to his great delight, that she was Ellie Lou Axson, the pastor's daughter and a talented artist whom everyone in the community loved and admired. She was in mourning because of the recent death of her mother.

"When I learned that this was Miss Ellie Lou Axson, of whom I had heard so often, quite a flood of light was let in on my understanding," Woodrow later wrote. "I took an early opportunity of calling on the Reverend Mr. Edward Axson. That dear gentleman received me with unsuspecting cordiality and sat down to entertain me under the impression I had come to see him." But Woodrow had come calling to see the minister's daughter. "I had not forgotten that pretty face and I wanted very much to see it again."

The smitten young Woodrow soon discovered that Miss Ellie Lou was much more than a pretty face. He also found her intelligent, funny, and thoughtful. "I had found a new and altogether delightful sort of companion." By the time he had met her again and gone for a walk in her company, "passion was beginning to enter into the criticism, and had pretty nearly gotten the better of it by the time we had climbed to the top of the hill." Woodrow Wilson had fallen in love.

Ellen Axson was equally attracted, but she resisted Woodrow's courtship because of her heavy family responsibilities. Her mother had died in childbirth two years before, and Ellen took care of her depressed and mentally ill father, two younger brothers, and her two-year-old sister.

Opposition to the romance came from Woodrow's father too; he thought his son should concentrate on his studies and on launching a career. But Woodrow knew Ellen was the right woman for him, and he was determined to let nothing stand in his way. He visited Rome two more times that summer and wrote her a series of passionate letters. He promised to take responsibility for her brothers and sister.

That September, as he was traveling to Baltimore, where he had been accepted in a program of study for a doctoral degree in history and political science at Johns Hopkins, he changed trains in Asheville, North Carolina. In a remarkable coincidence that they would both later attribute to divine intervention, Ellen was also in Asheville, waiting for a train to Rome. She had been on a visit to friends but had been called home because her father was very sick.

Woodrow spotted Ellen sitting in a hotel and rushed up to her. Both of them were stunned with surprise, but Woodrow proposed on the spot and Ellen accepted. There was hardly time to do more than give her a brief, sweet kiss before he had to hurry away to catch his train. When he arrived in Baltimore, Woodrow Wilson was engaged.

Although he didn't find life at Johns Hopkins perfect, he began to feel he had made the right choice. "Like everybody else I have learned chiefly by means of big mistakes. It took me all my college days to learn that it was necessary and profitable to study. Having made that tardy discovery, I left college on the wrong tack. I had then, as I have still, a very earnest political creed and very pronounced political ambitions," he wrote to Ellen. "But a man has to know the world before he can work in it to any purpose. He has to know the forces with which he must cooperate and those with which he must contend; must know how and where he can make himself felt. . . . He must know the times into which he has been born: and this I did *not* know when I left college and chose my profession."

So for two more years he prepared diligently for his new choice of a profession. He attended classes and seminars, sang with the glee club and became a leader in the literary society, studied, debated, made new friends, and wrote long, loving letters to Ellen. He also wrote a book called *Congressional Government*, based on his study of political legislative systems, and published a number of magazine articles on political and historical subjects.

As his studies at Johns Hopkins drew to a close, he lined up a job as a professor of history at a new college for women in Pennsylvania, Bryn Mawr. On June 24, 1885, Woodrow Wilson married Ellen Axson in a quiet evening ceremony jointly conducted by Ellen's grandfather and Woodrow's father in the parlor of a Presbyterian manse in Savannah, Georgia. They honeymooned at a small woodland resort in North Carolina and that fall settled in Bryn Mawr, where the twenty-eight-year-old Dr. Woodrow Wilson would begin his teaching career and achieve financial independence for the first time.

Ellen quickly became the anchor Woodrow needed, taking over all the details of daily life and freeing him to pursue his studies, teaching, and writing. The young couple spent a contented three years at Bryn Mawr, even though the professor felt that his abilities were somewhat wasted in the teaching of women, because they couldn't vote and he wanted to influence politics by inspiring his students. Dr. Wilson's lectures were popular, and he continued to write successfully. Margaret, the first of Woodrow and Ellen's three daughters, was born in April of 1886. A second daughter, Jessie, came along in 1887.

Early in the spring of 1888, Woodrow faced the first real tragedy of his life when his mother died in Clarksville, Tennessee, where his father had become a professor of divinity at Tennessee University. "As the first shock and acute pain of the great, the irreparable blow passes off, my heart is filling up with tenderest memories," he wrote to Ellen in a moving tribute, both to her and to his mother. "My mother, with her sweet womanliness, her purity, her intelligence, her strength, prepared me for my wife. I remember how I clung to her (a laughed-at 'Mamma's boy') till I was a great big fellow: but love of the best womanhood came to my heart through those apron strings."

Later that year, the thirty-one-year-old Woodrow Wilson was offered a professorship at Wesleyan University in Connecticut. There Dr. Wilson spread his wings. He founded a student debating club modeled on the British parliamentary system, became coach of the football team, which had its best season under his guidance, and taught lively courses in government and history.

He also became the father of a third daughter, Eleanor, who was born in 1889. There was some disappointment that the new baby was another girl, because everyone had been hoping for a boy, but Woodrow told Ellen that "no child of ours shall be unwelcome."

After another happy year at Wesleyan, Professor Woodrow Wilson received an irresistible new job offer, this one at the College of New Jersey in Princeton, his alma mater. Soon he and Ellen, along with their three little girls and Ellen's brother and sister, moved to the lovely college town that would be their home for the next two decades.

4

President of Princeton

Woodrow Wilson and Princeton were perfect for each other, each poised for important growth in new directions. Wilson came from the same staunch Presbyterian stock that had created Princeton, but he was bursting with new ideas about education and the role of universities in a changing society. Princeton was still small, with academic standards that needed upgrading. Both were ready to grow together.

Dr. Wilson had once told his wife that college lectures and classes were too often dull because the professors didn't have the imagination or the will to inspire their students. "Perfunctory lecturing is of no service," he said. Professor Wilson's lectures were never perfunctory. He managed to convey his enthusiasm to his students and injected a sense of excitement into the courses he taught. Soon he was one of the most popular teachers at Princeton. Students jammed the lecture halls to hear him and frequently broke into applause. He used his exceptional oratory, his passion for ideas, his solid reasoning, his provocative style, his quick wit, and his ability to stimulate student debate to turn the courses he taught into unforgettable learning experiences.

"His lectures held me spellbound" was a typical student comment. "I could never stop to take notes for fear of missing something."

"I consider Wilson the greatest classroom lecturer I have ever heard," a fellow professor said. "This is my mature conviction after experience in my school, college, and university life."

The president's residence at Princeton University in New Jersey. (The Library of Congress)

Wilson's reputation as a teacher spread. So did his reputation as a scholar and as the writer of books and magazine articles. He received many offers from other universities. The trustees at Princeton offered him a higher salary, much more than other professors were getting, in order to keep their most popular teacher.

Dr. Wilson and his family were content at Princeton, where he was by far the most popular campus figure. Although he had a reputation as a stern and somber individual, at home he was a lighthearted family man who romped with his three small daughters and entertained them by doing hilarious impressions. He organized games of charades, told funny stories, played tag. There were quiet times too, peaceful moments when he read aloud to his family, much like the times he remembered from his own childhood.

During this time, Woodrow Wilson pushed himself hard to maintain a relentless schedule of lecturing and writing. His drive was rooted partly in his perfectionism and the urgency to excel that had been with him since childhood and partly in the need for extra income. Although he managed to accomplish more in a day than most men, Wilson depended heavily on his wife and family to keep life running smoothly.

The demanding pace took a toll on his always precarious health. Ellen Wilson insisted that he needed a rest and urged him to take a vacation. Because their funds were limited and Ellen didn't want to leave the children, Woodrow went alone on his first trip to Europe and spent a long summer exploring England and Scotland by bicycle, visiting the places his ancestors had come from and the sites of his literary and political heroes' accomplishments. He also visited the great universities at Oxford and Cambridge, where he was impressed by the richness of academic life and the methods of teaching.

He returned, refreshed, to the Princeton campus, which was gearing up for the celebration of its 150th anniversary. During the three-day-long sesquicentennial festivities, Wilson marched enthusiastically in a torchlight procession down Nassau Street, partied exuberantly with the students, and gave the keynote speech, entitled "Princeton in the Nation's Service."

"It was the most brilliant, dazzling success from first to last," Ellen Wilson wrote about the speech. "And *such* an ovation as Woodrow received! I never imagined anything like it. And think of *so* delighting *such* an audience, the most distinguished, everyone says, that was ever assembled in America—famous men from all parts of Europe."

Religion continued to be a major force in Wilson's life. He regularly led his family in Bible reading, discussion, and prayer, much as his father had done when he was a little boy. His later efforts as a peacemaker and conciliator were predicted in his choice of a church to join. There were two Presbyterian churches in Princeton. They once had been a single congregation but had splintered over a dispute. Woodrow and Ellen joined the Second Presbyterian Church in 1897, and Woodrow

Woodrow Wilson, president of Princeton University, in 1902. (The Library of Congress)

was elected a ruling elder shortly afterward. Right away he tried to convince his fellow church members to put aside their differences and unite with the congregation of the First Presbyterian Church. He failed in this effort, though, and eventually changed his membership to the First Presbyterian Church.

Wilson's stature grew. He became the most influential person on the faculty and used his prestige to advocate improvements in the college curriculum. When members of the faculty clashed with the conservative university president, they often turned to Dr. Wilson for support. Eventually the president decided to resign, and it seemed natural for the board of trustees to turn to the popular and prestigious Professor Woodrow Wilson to replace him.

After serving as a professor for twelve years and attracting international acclaim, Wilson accepted the leadership of Princeton, becoming its first president who was not a clergyman. His colorful and tradition-rich inauguration ceremony on October 25, 1902, was attended by hundreds of visiting dignitaries, including former U.S. president Grover Cleveland, Robert T. Lincoln, son of Abraham Lincoln, Booker T. Washington, Mark Twain, financier J. P. Morgan, the governor of New Jersey, the presidents of dozens of colleges and universities, journalists, writers, and many members of his own Princeton class of 1879. One of his classmates joked that he was there for "the coronation of Tommy Wilson."

Another person there that day was magazine editor George Harvey, who had come with J. P. Morgan. Harvey had heard about Wilson and was impressed with the way he spoke. This man was suitable to be not only president of a university, Harvey thought, he could be president of the country.

One who listened to Woodrow Wilson that day with intense interest and glowing pride was the elderly and infirm Rev. Dr. Joseph Wilson, who had moved in with his son's family. In spite of pain and weakness, Dr. Wilson insisted on attending the ceremony. Not long afterward the old man suffered a heart attack that left him bedridden for the next few months. Even though Woodrow had many pressing duties, he found time almost every evening to sit with his father and talk or read aloud. When Dr. Wilson died on January 21, 1903, a month before his eighty-first birthday, death was viewed as a merciful release, because he had suffered a great deal at the end.

When Woodrow Wilson assumed the presidency of Princeton, he immediately set out to turn the provincial college into a first-rate university. "Princeton must challenge the supremacy of Harvard and Yale," he said. He planned a bold new way to teach undergraduates, the preceptorial system, by which students would live and interact in intimate groups with special teachers, preceptors, who would provide the kind of stimulating atmosphere needed to help students reach higher standards of learning and performance. He planned a new school of science, a graduate school, a law school, a school of electrical engineering, and a museum of natural science. Then he went to the board of trustees and asked for a staggering sum of money, more than $6 million, to turn these dreams into reality.

Although his plans were revolutionary for this staid institution, the faculty and trustees supported him, and Wilson worked with zeal to transform Princeton. The first thing he did was implement the preceptorial system, which was based on the tutorial system used at England's famous Oxford University. "If we could get a body of such tutors at Princeton, we could transform the place from a place where there are youngsters doing tasks to a place where there are men thinking, men who are conversing about the things of thought," Wilson said. Within a few short years, the preceptorial system, refined and adapted to circumstances at Princeton, was in place, with many of the young teachers personally recruited by Wilson.

Wilson also raised academic standards, making it much more difficult to get accepted at Princeton and much more rigorous to attend. He reorganized the academic departments and established requirements for broad liberal studies. When an influential man appealed to Wilson on behalf of an applicant who had not passed the entrance exam, Wilson turned him down

Woodrow Wilson and his wife Ellen Axson Wilson outside the president's residence at Princeton. (The Library of Congress)

flat. "I want you to understand," he said, "that if the angel Gabriel applied for admission to Princeton University and could not pass the entrance examinations, he would not be admitted. He would be wasting his time."

Wilson's ambitious goals and demanding pace of work placed stress on his health, and once again he found solace and recuperation in travel. In 1906 he suffered a small stroke and temporarily lost the sight in one eye. At first it looked as if he might have to retire to save his health, but the damage turned out not to be so severe. He did need rest, though, so he took his family on an extended vacation in England and Scotland, leaving before graduation and returning in the fall, invigorated and full of fresh plans and innovative ideas.

Wilson, though, was pushing the limits of his colleagues' and the trustees' tolerance for sweeping change and growth. Some felt he was pressing too hard, moving too fast. A few were jealous of his phenomenal success. Many honestly disagreed with him about some of the issues he had raised and plans he had made. "Wilson never knew when to stop," a friend of his said.

Once he had introduced the preceptorial system, reorganized the curriculum, tightened discipline, raised the level of scholarship, and instituted academic reforms, Wilson turned to the social side of life at Princeton, with a plan to extend the concepts of the preceptorial system by building a series of quadrangular buildings around central courts. Students and unmarried faculty members would live, eat, and study in their quads, part of a harmonious and stimulating adacemic community. Like his successful preceptorial program, the quadrangle or college plan had its roots in distinguished British universities, Wilson explained to the trustees. At first the plan made sense to the trustees, who quickly approved it.

The quadrangle plan had grown, in part, from Wilson's distress at the growing social importance of Princeton's exclusive off-campus eating clubs. Fraternities weren't allowed at Princeton, but the eating clubs served a similar function, giving

Woodrow Wilson in 1903. (The Library of Congress)

students a subgroup to identify with. During Wilson's own student days, the clubs had been fairly modest establishments where students gathered for meals. He had belonged to one himself, the Alligators. But the imposing buildings that lined Prospect Avenue in the small village of Princeton now served as exclusive enclaves for wealthy students. The eating clubs were snobbish and demoralizing, Wilson believed. The quadrangle plan would eliminate them.

As soon as the quad plan, as it came to be known, was announced, it generated fierce debate. Members of the eating clubs, hundreds of influential Princeton graduates, and many faculty members expressed strong opposition. Other faculty members, quite a few students, and many public leaders supported the idea. Soon the plan was the vortex of a tornado of controversy.

Although Wilson battled hard for his plan, influential alumni, many of them vital financial contributors, pressured the trustees until they withdrew their initial approval. They left Wilson an opportunity to work for some sort of a compromise plan. But compromise wasn't in Wilson's character, and the plan died. Ironically, although the idea was defeated at Princeton, it was eventually adopted at Harvard and other prestigious universities. The fight also attracted the attention of the press, which portrayed Wilson as the "champion of the underprivileged and the supporter of democratic principles."

The withdrawal of the quadrangle plan was a bitter defeat for Woodrow Wilson to accept, but another Princeton battle was shaping up, one that was even more unpleasant, one that would ultimately result in his decision to leave. Here is where Wilson's inability to accept any form of personal opposition first proved a serious threat to his leadership capability. Although he had been popular and successful at Princeton, Wilson's unyielding style had caused some friction, jealousy, and enmity. One of those whose opposition he had aroused was Professor Andrew West, dean of Princeton's graduate school.

Wilson had long wanted to expand the graduate programs

and decided that the best way to do so was to build a new graduate school complex at the center of the university campus. "Wilson didn't want a hundred nice young men to come to Princeton and live apart pursuing the higher culture," one sympathetic colleague of his said. "His thought was aflame with the picture of a great democratic society of students in which undergraduates and postgraduates should meet and mingle with healthy clashes of mind on mind."

Dean West, however, wanted the new graduate school to be built at a separate location so that the graduate students could live and study in a more elite atmosphere, undistracted by the undergraduate programs. West actively opposed Wilson's plans. Because the new school would have to be funded by contributions from wealthy philanthropists, West urged potential donors to make their gifts contingent on the separate graduate school.

When the owner of a major company offered half a million dollars for an off-campus graduate center of the type West preferred, Wilson denounced the proposed gift in stinging terms. "I cannot accede to the acceptance of gifts upon terms which take the educational policy of the university out of the hands of the trustees and faculty and permit it to be determined by those who give money," he said. The insulted business magnate withdrew the offer. Professor West immediately complained to trustees and influential alumni. The resulting outcry generated even more of a storm than Wilson's quadrangle proposal had. A movement to oust Wilson started to grow.

The embattled Princeton president decided to take his argument directly to the alumni. He toured the country, speaking to groups of graduates. Was higher education to be controlled by the wealthy? he asked. Would democracy or riches rule? "The American college must become saturated in the same sympathies as the common people," he said. "The American people will tolerate nothing that savors of political exclusiveness. Their political parties are going to pieces. Only those leaders who seem able to promise something of a moral advance are able to secure a following. The people are tired of pretense, and I ask you as Princeton men to heed what is going on."

Wilson's skill as a persuasive orator brought him a victory when the board of trustees announced its support of his position. But the victory was short-lived. Shortly after the trustees' vote of confidence, a wealthy Massachusetts man died and left $5 million for the Princeton graduate school. Dean West was named as trustee for the estate.

Wilson got the news in a telegram, which he showed to his wife. "See this," he said. "We have beaten the living, but we cannot fight the dead!"

5

Governor of New Jersey

Woodrow Wilson's radical, impressive, and stormy presidency of Princeton University made him a well-known public figure. His battles over the quadrangle system and the graduate school generated a great deal of attention in the press. His books and articles were favorably received and widely read. Many people were impressed with Wilson's clear thinking and lofty ideals.

Ironically, it was his conservative views that gave Woodrow Wilson, later a hero of liberals, his opportunity for a career in politics. Among his admirers was George Harvey, an influential conservative Democrat, friend of millionaires, and editor of *Harper's Weekly*, a conservative magazine. Harvey had heard Wilson's inaugural speech at Princeton. He liked what Wilson had said and believed him to be a fellow conservative. He recognized Wilson's ability to sway audiences with his speeches and thought that he was a man people would vote for. He saw in Woodrow Wilson a potential president of the country, one who would be far, far better than the man he feared would eventually win the presidency.

Harvey and other conservative Democrats were afraid that William Jennings Bryan, and enormously popular progressive politician, would be the Democratic nominee in 1912 and, in the changing mood of the times, might actually win. Harvey and his fellow conservatives considered Bryan's populist ideas dangerously radical. Harvey also relished the role of kingmaker, the chance to use his influence to elevate a protégé to power.

At about the time Wilson's problems at Princeton were leading him to consider resignation, the Democratic party in the state of New Jersey, where Princeton is located, was facing poor prospects in the upcoming election for governor. New Jersey was a state where party bosses controlled elections and where big businesses found a haven from laws and regulations. Naturally, business interests opposed the kinds of reforms that populists and progressives from both major parties were calling for.

Harvey suggested Wilson as a possible candidate for governor to the party boss, an old-fashioned "machine" politician named James "Big Jim" Smith. The Democratic party needed candidates capable of attracting votes in the changing times. Voters were becoming aware of the corruption of the political bosses and the growing power of big business. They were calling for reform in ever increasing numbers, their demands fed by the populist, socialist, and progressive movements.

Woodrow Wilson seemed like the kind of candidate Smith and Harvey were looking for, one who could sway voters but who was conservative enough not to be a threat to big business. They thought his idealism was an act. No one could really be that naive, they told each other.

Wilson, who had never lost his interest in political issues and had followed them closely during his academic years, considered himself a conservative Democrat. On more than one occasion he had professed scorn for the progressive ideas of William Jennings Bryan, although, as a Democrat, he had voted for him in 1900 and 1908. He had been intrigued by the flamboyant progressive Republican Theodore Roosevelt, although he didn't agree with many of Roosevelt's ideas. Wilson's conservative views, however, were motivated not by the greed typical of many special interest groups but by idealism.

He was definitely the product of his southern background and his staunch religious upbringing. For example, his views on the roles of women and blacks in society were somewhat patronizing, if kindly motivated, and he had been sheltered from the brutal realities of devastating social problems such as

Wilson on the campaign trail. (The Library of Congress)

poverty and child labor, so he hadn't given them much thought.
He genuinely enjoyed his stimulating intellectual life-style and
had no reason to question the traditional political values
shared by many of those from his background.

The controversies at Princeton, though, had made him won-
der if reformers who claimed that the forces of wealth and
privilege were incompatible with democracy might be right.
Still, even with his increasing awareness of the excesses of
entrenched wealth and special interests and the public outcry
against things such as protective tariffs and monopolies, the
Woodrow Wilson of 1910 seemed safe and respectable to the
conservatives who were maneuvering to make him governor of
New Jersey as a step on the road to the White House.

Wilson was nominated for governor in September of 1910 at
the state Democratic party convention as a result of the support of Boss Jim Smith and the conservative Democrats who
represented big business interests. Wilson's nomination was

Wilson's long fascination with the art of oratory made him an out-standing public speaker, able to reach people with clearly expressed ideas. (The Library of Congress)

actively opposed by liberal or progressive Democrats who believed in reform and were sure that Wilson was under the control of those who had supported him.

When he arrived at the convention to make his acceptance speech, he was introduced as "the candidate for the governorship and the next president of the United States." The politicos and bosses cheered, but the progressives waited in grim silence, frustrated at their inability to discredit Wilson and prevent his nomination.

The unhappy insurgents, as the progressives were often called, took heart, though, at what came next. "I did not seek this nomination," Wilson said in an electrifying speech. "It has come to me absolutely unsolicited." The nominee then promised that "I shall enter the duties of the office of Governor, if elected, with absolutely no pledge of any kind to prevent me from serving the people of the state."

This promise was greeted with smiles all around. The bosses and conservatives smiled because they thought it was just campaign rhetoric. The progressives were pleasantly surprised at the ring of conviction in his speech. All of them had misjudged their candidate.

One of those who had worked the hardest in the unsuccessful effort to prevent Wilson from getting the nomination was a young man named Joseph Tumulty. He found the speech so inspiring that he was instantly converted from opponent to ardent supporter. He immediately volunteered to work on Wilson's campaign and eventually became the governor's secretary.

Once nominated, Wilson focused his considerable abilities and all his energy on winning the election. Here is where his intellectual skill came into play; he was easily able to grasp issues and understand the implications of various positions. Here, too, his powerful speaking ability would serve him well.

As he studied the issues, Wilson realized that it would be necessary to advocate reform. The nation was ripe for the changes that populists, progressives, and insurgents were call-

Although he was new to the hurly-burly of running for public office, Wilson found that campaigning agreed with him and that he was quite good at it. (The Library of Congress)

ing for. Farmers in the West and South were the victims of low crop prices and unfair banking practices. Waves of immigrants were being exploited as cheap labor, displacing other Americans from their jobs. Almost 2 million of the nation's workers were children under age sixteen, many of whom toiled long hard hours under brutal conditons for pittance wages. The growing cities of the Northeast were filled with tenements teeming with immigrants.

Meanwhile, as the poor grew poorer, a handful of rich company owners grew ever richer and more powerful, with banking, utilities, transportation, and other big businesses in the hands of a few enormously wealthy men. Legislatures and the courts were controlled by political bosses, who were in turn controlled by big business magnates.

As governor of New Jersey, Wilson attended many ceremonial func-
tions. (The Library of Congress)

New Jersey was rampant with the worst excesses of the
business practices opposed by reformers. Voters wanted
change, and the reformers were willing to give it to them. At the
top of the reformers' list was the need for government regulation of utilities, railroads, business, and industry. They were
also calling for an overhaul of the political system to reduce
the influence of the political bosses, and they wanted direct
election of senators. (In New Jersey senators were appointed by
the state legislature, which was, of course, under machine
control.)

Wilson turned out to be an effective campaigner and an
articulate voice that reached the voters. "If I am elected, I shall
have been elected leader of my party and governor of all the
people of New Jersey to conduct government in their interest

and in their interest only," he told a cheering crowd in one campaign speech. "If the Democratic Party does not understand it that way, then I want to say to you very frankly that the Democratic Party ought not to elect me governor!"

Wilson campaigned on a four-point program, promising to push for new laws to eliminate government and business corruption, ensure compensation for workers who were injured on the job, provide for nomination of candidates for office by direct primary, and, most important, institute regulation of public utilities and transportation.

Experienced politicians didn't think he would be able to convince the legislature to enact such radical reforms, but voters responded enthusiastically. On election day they gave Wilson an overwhelming victory, with the largest margin of votes ever captured by a Democratic candidate in this Republican state. He also swept enough other Democrats into office with him to give the party control of the state assembly for the first time in many years.

After this stunning victory, he immediately set out on his own course, as he had said he would do. In the process, he stunned the bosses. The first showdown came right after the election.

In New Jersey, the state legislature was supposedly guided in its choice of senators by a nonbinding "preference primary" in which party members indicated their senatorial choices. James E. Martine had won the primary.

Boss Smith had served in the senate once before but had lost his position when Republicans won control in New Jersey. In the 1910 election, he had not entered the preference primary because of "health reasons." The day after Wilson's election victory and Martine's winning of the preference primary, Big Jim Smith went to see the governor-elect. He offered hearty congratulations to Wilson, then told him that there had been a miraculous improvement in his health, so he was "yielding to the wishes of his friends to have the State Legislature appoint him to the United States Senate."

The Wilson family. From left to right, Margaret, Ellen Axson Wilson, Eleanor, Jessie, and Woodrow Wilson. (The Library of Congress)

Although Wilson wasn't enthusiastic about Martine, he had pledged his support to the winner of the primary and had promised throughout his campaign to listen to the voice of the people. He told Smith that Martine should get the job.

"The primary is a joke!" Big Jim responded.

"It is far from a joke with me," the outraged Wilson replied. He understood that his entire political future would depend on the outcome of this first battle, so he plunged into a furious effort to defeat Smith's senatorial bid in the legislature. For two months he contacted members of the assembly. He sent satements to newspapers and made endless speeches. The idea was to put so much public pressure on the representatives that

The summer residence of the New Jersey governor at Sea Girt, New Jersey. (The Library of Congress)

they would find the courage to vote with Wilson and against the machine.

The battle ended when the legislature picked Martine. Wilson was now firmly in control of the Democratic party in New Jersey. He earned the growing respect of progressives all over the country. After his inauguration as governor on January 17, 1911, he set out to build on his reputation by keeping his campaign promises.

Doing so meant getting the legislature to pass some controversial new laws. Although a majority of the assembly representatives were Democrats and Wilson's position had been strengthened by the senatorial defeat of Boss Smith, the machine politicians still wielded considerable influence. Bitter at what they considered Wilson's opportunistic about-face, they were determined to use their remaining clout to humiliate him. In the state senate, the Republicans still held a slim majority. Here, Wilson's task would require even more adroit political maneuvering.

Wilson was growing into a deft politician, though, and he took a series of masterful steps to push his programs through both houses of the legislature. His new personal secretary, Joseph Tumulty, advised him to entertain state senate leaders of both parties and to do his best to overcome his stiff shyness with strangers. Tumulty urged him to allow the warm and humorous side of his personality, which his family and close associates knew, to show through his normally reserved style. Wilson and Tumulty decided to create as relaxed and informal an atmosphere as possible and invited the prominent politicians to a stag dinner at a country club. The party turned into a "smashing success."

"The senators are as jolly as boys when they let themselves go," Wilson said of the evening, which he characterized "as one unbroken romp" that was highlighted by humorous speeches, witty repartee, boisterous dancing, and high glee.

To help win the support of Republicans, Wilson enlisted a respected Republican progressive to write the reform laws he hoped to persuade the legislature to enact. He met directly with lawmakers of both parties. He sought the support of progressives from both parties and used the full force of his personality, his commanding oratorical skill, and his ability to rally the press and public opinion, putting such intense pressure on reluctant lawmakers that they capitulated. In a little over a month, Wilson shepherded a sweeping series of new laws through New Jersey's legislature.

The first was a law requiring nomination of party candidates by primary elections, designed to incapacitate the boss system and reduce the influence of the political machines. Big Jim Smith and his cohorts fought the bill bitterly, but Wilson's skillful efforts resulted in victory.

Piece after piece of reform legislation was passed. One new law established a strong public utilities commission to fix rates, set standards, and regulate the business practices of railroad and power, water and telephone companies. Another law decimated the power of the bosses by allowing cities to choose a commission form of government. Workers injured on the job were protected under the provisions of a workmen's compensation act that held employers liable for employee injuries. Laws were passed that regulated child labor, established safety requirements for the processing of food, and reorganized the public schools.

Political success delighted Wilson. "I got absolutely everything I strove for and more besides," he told a friend. "I kept the pressure of opinion constantly on the legislature." Exultant in victory, the governor decided that politics agreed with him. "It's a great game, thoroughly worth playing!" he said.

6

The Way to the White House

Woodrow Wilson's astonishing success in his first months as governor of New Jersey encouraged those who had been thinking of him as a presidential prospect to set their plans in motion. A group of influential Democratic supporters formed a preliminary campaign organization in early 1911 and began to seek support for a Wilson candidacy from key Democratic factions across the country.

Although Wilson had been active in politics for only a short time, the national political situation was encouraging for several reasons. The progressive movement that had swept the country for the past twenty years had created radical changes in party politics. The Republicans were bitterly divided between those who supported former president Teddy Roosevelt, a progressive pioneer, and the conservatives, who remained loyal to Roosevelt's ineffective successor, President William Howard Taft.

William Jennings Bryan had been the undisputed progressive leader of the Democratic party and its dominant force since 1896, but the days of his prime influence were waning, and he had already announced that he would not be a candidate in 1912. There weren't any entrenched Democratic leaders of national stature, so the field was wide open for a promising newcomer such as Woodrow Wilson.

Woodrow Wilson's national presidential campaign headquarters opened in the fall of 1911 in New York City. (The Library of Congress)

Wilson's early supporters sent him on a speaking tour. He traveled throughout the West and South, discussing problems of state and local government, endorsing reform of the political process, and winning the support of many progressives. His popularity with those he met convinced both him and his advisers to announce his candidacy and pursue the nomination. In November of 1911, Wilson's national campaign headquarters opened in New York.

At first it looked as if the popular and articulate Woodrow Wilson would be unbeatable, but the betrayed party bosses and the conservatives he had alienated in his swing to progressivism made a massive effort to discredit him. Meanwhile, several other Democratic contenders emerged.

When the Democratic party held its nominating convention in late June of 1912, more than a thousand delegates gathered

During the long battle for the nomination, Wilson waited at Sea Girt, where he made his acceptance speech. (The Library of Congress)

in Baltimore, Maryland, to choose the presidential candidate. The race had boiled down to a probable choice between Wilson and James "Champ" Clark, Speaker of the House of Representatives and a longtime supporter of Bryan, with an Alabama conservative, Oscar Underwood, as an outside possibility.

Clark seemed the likeliest victor, but after days of furious behind-the-scenes activities and political horse trading, no one garnered enough votes on the first ballot to win the nomination. Champ Clark came out ahead of Wilson, but, in ballot after ballot, he was unable to muster the two-thirds majority necessary for nomination. The struggle continued for day after exhausting day. On the tenth ballot, the New York political machine shifted to Clark. Wilson's supporters were desolate, fearing a stampede. It looked like the campaign would soon be over.

Wilson's oratorical skill was a major factor in winning him the Democratic presidential nomination and the election. (The Library of Congress)

At the New Jersey governor's residence at Sea Girt, where Wilson calmly awaited the convention news, the postman brought an undertaker's catalog with the morning mail. "This is certainly prompt service," Wilson joked to his family. "Will you help me choose a coffin for a dead duck?"

The expected stampede didn't materialize, though. On the fourteenth ballot, the bosses' endorsement of Clark backfired when William Jennings Bryan switched his support to Wilson because of it. Wilson's vote count increased slightly. The balloting continued. After the twenty-fifth ballot, Wilson made another joke. "I've been figuring that at the present rate of gain, I'll be nominated on 175 more ballots."

On the thirtieth ballot, Wilson passed Clark. On the forty-second ballot, Wilson won a majority. Support for Clark ebbed, and a Wilson stampede began to build. Delegates, even those who didn't really like Wilson, began to believe that he now had the best chance to wrest the presidency from the Republicans. It took forty-six ballots, but Wilson won.

Although Wilson was a real spellbinder, he appealed to voters' ideals rather than to their emotions. (The Library of Congress)

Meanwhile, the Republicans nominated President Taft. The flamboyant Theodore Roosevelt and his supporters decided to form their own party, the Progressive or Bull Moose party, with Roosevelt, of course, as their candidate. The Republican split left the door wide open for the Democrats to regain the White House for the first time since Grover Cleveland had been president.

Taft never really had a chance. The contest was between Roosevelt and Wilson. The magnetic Roosevelt campaigned hard for his "New Nationalism," which blended an appeal to patriotism with the classic progressivism of the Midwest. He proposed the creation of a government commission to regulate huge corporations and monopolies.

Wilson called his program for progressive reform the "New Freedom." Big business and wealthy financiers had controlled both government and the Republican party for too long, Wilson claimed. With a platform shrewdly designed to appeal to all the factions of the Democratic party as well as to disenchanted progressive Republicans, he advocated giving control of the government back to the people—the farmers, laborers, shopkeepers, and hardworking citizens of America's cities and rural areas—by breaking up massive companies and restoring traditional competition.

Actually, there wasn't a great deal of difference between Wilson and Roosevelt on the major progressive issue, correcting the rampant abuses of big business. Both candidates thought government regulation and control of some sort were necessary. It was really a matter of degree, with Wilson's approach slightly more cautious and moderate. "I don't want the American economy enslaved by a few wealthy czars, but I don't want government regulation that will enslave us," he said.

Wilson's New Freedom platform positioned him advantageously between the conservative Taft and the radical Roosevelt. Although he didn't get a majority of the popular vote in the November general election, the split in the Republican party gave Wilson an overwhelming victory in the electoral college.

A jubilant president-to-be boards a special Washington-bound train in Princeton, after having been given a rousing send-off. (The Library of Congress)

The final popular vote was 6,300,000 for Wilson to 4,100,000 for Roosevelt and a humiliating 3,480,000 for Taft. Woodrow Wilson, the political newcomer who had evolved from conservative to progressive in a few short years, would be going to the White House.

When word of the victory reached Princeton, the bell at Nassau Hall on the university campus began to ring. Students and townspeople thronged the streets and congregated happily in front of the Wilson home. The new president-elect climbed onto a chair on the front porch and gave a brief, impromptu speech. "I myself have no feeling of triumph tonight," Wilson told the cheering supporters. "I have a feeling of solemn responsibility."

The next morning Wilson, triumphant but tired, met with reporters. "I am through with statements. I am now going to do some hard thinking," he told them. The busy house in Princeton wasn't conducive for such meditation, though. Wilson was immediately swamped with requests from politicians all over

Outgoing president William Howard Taft and president-elect Woodrow Wilson ride together to Wilson's inauguration. (The Library of Congress)

the country for appointment to public office. He was deluged by the press and besieged by representatives of all sorts of groups who now wanted to establish influence in the new administration.

Wilson decided to get away for a respite from the demands and pressure. He announced that no appointments would be made until he had returned from a vacation to Bermuda with his wife and two of his daughters. He left the handling of political demands to a trusted adviser, Col. Edward House.

When they had met only a year before, House and Wilson had hit it off right away. House was a sincere admirer of Wilson as well as a capable and quiet adviser. He seemed to know intuitively how Wilson would want to approach a problem, and he had sound political instincts that would prove extremely useful in helping the new president to build an administration.

In Bermuda, Wilson worked in peace, approaching the choices that faced him in a characteristically methodical way. For cabinet positions, for example, he made a detailed chart listing the qualifications and background facts for each possible candidate. When he returned to the United States in December, he was rested and ready to tackle the challenges ahead. "We all feel ready for anything," he said.

During the early days of 1913, Wilson gradually pulled together his cabinet and announced a series of appointments. In making his choices, he relied heavily on the advice of Joe Tumulty, who had been with him since the campaign for governor, and on Colonel House, but the final decision was always his own. It wasn't easy to find the right people to serve in top-level government posts. The Democratic party had been out of office for so long that capable leaders who shared Wilson's progressive views were scarce. "I have been sweating blood over the cabinet choice," Wilson wrote to an old friend.

William Jennings Bryan, the great populist leader whose support had eventually helped Wilson get the nomination, was appointed secretary of state. William Gibbs McAdoo, a key member of the team that had engineered Wilson's election victory, was named secretary of the treasury. Wilson chose an old friend, Josephus Daniels, to be secretary of the navy and named an ambitious young New Yorker, Franklin Delano Roosevelt, to serve as assistant secretary of the navy.

Tumulty was named secretary to the president and made responsible for dealing with the press. Colonel House, although he held no official position, remained available as a counselor to the president, who relied especially on his expertise in foreign affairs. The new administration was finally in place, ready to lead the way into an era of reform.

The day before the inauguration, the Wilson family boarded a special train that took them to Washington after a rousing send-off in Princeton. The festivities were as simple and as pleasant as the Wilsons could make them. There was no elaborate inaugural ball, no massive parade, no unnecessary pomp, just a brief ceremony followed by a dignified, horse-drawn procession to the White House, where the new First Family hosted a modest buffet luncheon.

Still, a huge crowd gathered to watch Woodrow Wilson be sworn in on March 4, 1913. The short ceremony was held in front of the Capitol building, where Wilson repeated the oath of office to Chief Justice Edward D. White, his hand on his wife's Bible, which was open to Psalm 119. Then it was time to make his first speech as president.

The Secret Service had roped off a large open area between the president and the public. Wilson looked down from his podium and gestured to the agents. "Take down the ropes and let the people come forward," he said. The barricades were removed, and the enthusiastic crowd pressed closer.

"This is not a day of triumph," Wilson said in his short, stirring inaugural address. "It is a day of dedication. Here muster, not the forces of party, but the forces of humanity. Men's hearts wait upon us; men's lives hang in the balance; men's hopes call upon us to say what we will do. Who shall live up to the great trust? Who dares fail to try? I summon all honest men, all patriotic, all forward-looking men, to my side. God helping me, I will not fail them, if they will but counsel and sustain me!"

7

The New Freedom

Woodrow Wilson was an innovative president from the very beginning. He brought with him to the White House a clear idea of his role, one based on years of study and reflection. He had once believed that the president wielded little power. The real power, he had written in an early book, *Congressional Government,* was vested in the powerful congressional committee chairmen.

Since then he had decided the nation was dependent on a powerful president to serve as a "unifying force in our complex system, the leader of both his party and the nation." Determined to be such a leader, Wilson started his presidency with the same unorthodox and highly personal approach that had characterized his first year as governor of New Jersey.

He had been president for only a few weeks when he went to Congress and addressed a joint session, something that hadn't been done since the days of John Adams over a century before. Wilson wanted to show the senators and representatives, he said, that he was an approachable person rather than a lofty executive "hailing congress from some isolated island of jealous power."

Wilson's move was shrewdly calculated to help get his New Freedom legislative program passed by Congress, something he knew would be difficult. He was counting once again on the extraordinary mix of persuasion, personality, and public pressure that had been so successful in getting reform bills passed by the New Jersey legislature.

First Lady Ellen Axson Wilson. (The Library of Congress)

The First Family. Left to right, standing: Jessie and Eleanor (nick-named Nellie). Seated: Ellen Axson Wilson, Woodrow Wilson, and Margaret. (The Library of Congress)

Another Woodrow Wilson innovation was the presidential press conference. The president invited a hundred reporters to the East Room on March 15, 1913, and told them he would meet with them twice a week for a question-and-answer period. "I feel that a large part of the success of public affairs depends on the newspapermen because the news is the atmosphere of public affairs. Unless you get the right setting to affairs, disperse the right impression, things go wrong," he told them.

Soon after his historic visit to Congress, Wilson started presenting his New Freedom reforms. First came a bill that would reduce protective tariffs, fees imposed on imported products to make them more expensive for consumers than ones produced in the United States. Free trade versus protectionism was one of the hottest issues of the day.

Protectionists argued that high tariffs protected American companies against foreign competition. Free trade advocates said the tariffs protected inefficient American industries, causing higher prices for all Americans and damaging the overall economy for the benefit of a few wealthy investors.

Wilson had spoken out against protective tariffs during his campaign, and now he asked Congress to pass a bill that would bring down tariffs from an average of 40 percent to an average of 29 percent and would eliminate the tariffs altogether on a large number of products, including iron and steel, wool, sugar, shoes, clothing, and agricultural machinery.

The special interests responded with a furious campaign to defeat the bill or, at the very least, weaken it by amendments, so that individual industries would still have protection. An army of lobbyists descended on Washington, all determined to fight. There were so many, Wilson said, that "a brick couldn't be thrown without hitting one of them." He characterized the lobbyists as men who were seeking "to create an artificial opinion and overcome the interests of the public for their private profit" and called on the public to lobby for itself by communicating with representatives in Congress, demanding support of the bill. The public, stirred by Wilson's challenge, swamped senators and representatives with letters, calls, and telegrams.

Wilson also lobbied personally, pressuring individual senators in visits to the Capitol, holding party conferences, making telephone calls, giving public speeches, and writing letters. As Congress wrangled through the steamy summer of 1913, Wilson maintained the pressure by keeping the issue constantly in the press, speaking directly to the public, and working steadily behind the scenes to influence members of both the House of Representatives and the Senate. "The Senate is tired, some of the members of its Committee are irritable and will have to be indulged with a few days of rest, but there will be no insuperable difficulty in handling the situation as far as I can see," Wilson said of his strategy. The result of the long, tough fight

President Wilson poses with his loyal and capable personal secretary, Joseph Tumulty. (The Library of Congress)

was victory in September with the passage of the historic Underwood-Simmons Act.

As he had done in New Jersey, Wilson immediately followed up his triumph with another push. Congress wanted a break, but the president insisted it remain in session until it had passed his banking reform plan, another plank in the New Freedom platform.

There was no doubt that banks needed reforming. The question was exactly how to overhaul the system. Wilson had an important advantage as he tackled this thorny issue. He didn't have a plan of his own, so he was willing to consult with advocates of different programs and able to act as a buffer in the clash between conservatives, who wanted bankers to keep control of money, and progressives, who wanted a government-run banking system and money issued by the government.

Although Wilson agreed with many conservative points, the progressives insisted that the banking system be managed by a government commission and that new currency be backed by the government. The legislation proposed by the progressives wasn't exactly in the mode of the New Freedom, but Wilson decided to support it.

Once he had committed himself, Wilson held firm against conservatives and pushed hard for passage of the Federal Reserve Act. Opponents tried to stall, but the president kept up his relentless pressure. The struggle continued through late summer and fall. Wilson announced that there would be no Christmas break until there was a vote on the banking issue. Finally, on December 19, the act was passed.

Although the passages of the tariff and banking reform bills were major triumphs for the new president, they didn't do much to solve the biggest domestic problem facing the United States, the deadly monopolistic control of business and industry. In January of 1914, Wilson turned his energies to the passage of two landmark pieces of legislation, the Federal Trade Commission Act and the Clayton Anti-Trust Act.

Once again, there was a struggle with Congress that continued through the spring and summer. This time Wilson had to compromise, allowing amendments to weaken the antitrust bill and making some weak appointments to the new Federal Trade Commission in response to pressure from big business. But the new laws accomplished their basic purpose.

Wilson was most interested in his domestic programs. But, forced from the beginning to deal with a series of difficult international issues, he developed a bold new foreign policy based on honor and the denunciation of imperialism. "The United States will never again seek one additional foot of territory by conquest," he told the American people.

Fifteen years before, as the turn of the century approached, the United States had fought the brief Spanish-American War over control of Spanish colonies in the Western Hemisphere. America's great frontier era was now over, with the country's territory stretching from the Atlantic to the Pacific ocean. The response of some was to seek territory beyond the continental borders. This policy of imperialism, marked by the annexation of territories such as Guam, Hawaii, the Philippine Islands, and Puerto Rico and the control of native people who were not granted citizenship, was controversial. Some Americans believed that the United States should extend its benign influence beyond its borders. Others thought that the nation was in danger of becoming a colonial power. Wilson, like the isolationists, believed that such imperialism would lead to dangerous entanglements.

Wilson's new foreign policy was immediately tested in a series of crises. He took a tough stand against the so-called dollar diplomacy in China, where private bankers expected the government to use force, if necessary, against governments that didn't pay back loans.

He agreed to pay Colombia $25 million for the territory across which the United States had built the Panama Canal. "This nation can afford to be generous in the settling of disputes," he

Eleanor (left) and Jessie (right) both had White House weddings during President Wilson's hectic first term of office. (The Library of Congress)

said, "especially when by its generosity it can increase the friendliness of the many millions in Central and South America with whom our relations become daily more intimate."

In another dispute involving the Panama Canal, Wilson decided that Great Britain's protest against favorable tolls for American ships was valid. He pushed through Congress repeal of the Panama Canal Act, which had endorsed the favoritism.

Natives in the Philippines had been revolting against American rule ever since the Spanish-American War. In another controversial but courageous move, Wilson initiated a series of Philippine governmental changes that would lead to eventual independence.

The biggest test of Wilson's foreign policy came when a dictator seized power in Mexico. American business interests with valuable Mexican investments urged Wilson to recognize the dictator, but he refused. Eventually the president was forced to commit American troops and lives to resolve the crisis. For a while it looked as if the situation might lead to war, but Wilson's resolve was vindicated when Argentina, Brazil, and Chile, the "ABC Powers," offered to mediate. Wilson agreed to their intervention, resisting intense pressure at home to take advantage of the situation in order to capture territory in Mexico. The result was a new era of trust between the United States and its neighbor to the south.

President Wilson endured widespread castigation from an often hostile press for his foreign policy, but he managed to get off an occasional barb of his own. "It is an anxious business, but not impossible," he said of the situation in Mexico. "My head has never been as muddled about it as the heads of some editors seem to be."

The president's life wasn't all crisis management and struggling with Congress. In early July the White House announced the engagement of Jessie Wilson to Francis Sayre, an assistant district attorney in New York City, and a lovely White House wedding was held in November. It was a bittersweet occasion because it marked the first break in the close family circle. "I

need not tell you what effect it has had on our spirits to part
with her," Woodrow wrote to a friend. "But Ellen has acted with
noble unselfishness in hiding her distress and I have tried to
emulate her example."

The following May there was another wedding, this time of
Woodrow and Ellen's youngest daughter, Nellie, to the secretary
of the treasury "after a whirlwind courtship." Although William
McAdoo, a widower, was much older than their daughter, the
Wilsons didn't object, but they again felt the wrench of losing a
daughter. "The wedding was as simple and beautiful as any I
ever saw or imagined and she has married a noble man who will
make her happy and proud, too," the president said. "But just
now I can realize, in my selfishness, only that I have lost her,
for good and all."

All in all, Woodrow Wilson found the challenges, crises, and
pleasures of his first year in office demanding, stimulating, and
rewarding, even if, as he confided to Ellen, "the president is a
superior kind of slave." Being president was hard work, but it
agreed with him. "The days are so full of matters of conse-
quence and even anxiety that they count for quite four times
the hours they contain. And yet they have a certain relish in
them too. I would not have you think that it is all burden or that
the burden distresses. It is heavy, very heavy, but the strength
to carry it seems to go along with it." He would soon need every
ounce of strength that he could muster.

8

The Peace President

The first year of Woodrow Wilson's presidency was marked by achievement and reform, but clouds of tragedy loomed on the horizon. Wilson's greatest struggles, both personal and political, were yet to come.

For twenty-nine years, Ellen Axson Wilson had been the center of her husband's life, his personal anchor. She had created the peaceful and private home life that was essential to his health, both mental and physical. Together, she and Woodrow had raised three daughters and had shared a special closeness in such cherished privacy that the outside world rarely had a glimpse of it.

Now, though, while the winds of war were being fanned by conflict in Europe and America struggled in its emerging international role, Ellen Wilson lay in a stifling upstairs room in the White House struggling against a disease of the kidneys that made her progressively weaker.

Adm. Cary Grayson, the White House physician and a close personal friend, was deeply worried, both about Ellen's prognosis and about the dreadful effect her illness was having on the president. Ellen had been sick for several months. Numerous medical specialists had seen her, and Grayson had attended her almost around the clock. Grayson knew that hope was gone and that she was dying.

Wilson simply couldn't accept the reality of his wife's illness. He sat with her for hours at a time, holding her hand, praying for her recovery, almost trying to use the force of his will to revive her. As each hot July day passed, Ellen grew weaker. A sense of gloomy despair pervaded the White House.

The serene Ellen seemed to be the only one capable of accepting the truth; her concern was not for herself but for her husband. On the afternoon of August 6, 1914, she whispered to the doctor, "Take good care of Woodrow."

The doctor nodded and promised that he would.

Ellen clung to her husband's hand and rested for a few moments, exhausted by the struggle to speak. She looked into his eyes and summoned up enough energy to smile before closing her eyes and taking one last, shallow breath. Then she quietly died.

Woodrow Wilson was devastated. "God has stricken me almost beyond what I can bear," he wrote to a friend. Grief consumed him until he was numb with it.

There was no time for President Wilson to abandon himself to grief, though. As Ellen Wilson had lain dying in the White House, the nations of Europe had been plunged into a devastating war.

The immediate cause was the assassination of Archduke Franz Ferdinand, heir to the throne of Austria-Hungary, by a Serbian terrorist on June 28, 1914. Most Americans were hardly aware of the death of an obscure European aristocrat, but the incident set off a chain of events so that by August most of Europe was at war. The Central Powers of Germany, Austria-Hungary, and Turkey were aligned on one side and the Allies of Great Britain, France, and Russia on the other.

Wilson fervently believed that the United States had no place in this war and wanted a policy of strict American neutrality. He worried that because the United States was a nation of immigrants, many Americans would identify with the nations from which they or their ancestors had come. "The United States must be neutral in fact as well as in name," he told the Senate in mid-August. "We must be impartial in thought as well as in action, must put a curb upon our sentiments."

President Wilson was devastated by the death of his first wife, Ellen Louise Axson Wilson, affectionately known as Miss Ellie Lou. (The Library of Congress)

Such impartiality of thought proved easier said than done. Wilson himself came from a strong British background, and he was naturally inclined to think of Germany as a militaristic aggressor, especially after Germany invaded Belgium, a neutral country. Many other American individuals and businesses, including powerful investors whose lucrative trade with Britain

Both Jessie and Nellie presented the president with grandchildren during his first term of office. Sadly, Ellen Wilson died before their births. Here the president holds his granddaughter Ellen Wilson McAdoo, named for his beloved first wife. (The Library of Congress)

When concerned family and friends introduced Edith Bolling Galt to the grieving president, they were delighted to see the romance "take." (The Library of Congress)

meant an important economic stake in the war, were also instinctively inclined to favor the Allies. American banks also had important British connections and played a vital role in financing the Allied war effort. The role of American business made the nation's strict neutrality doubtful from the beginning. Other Americans sympathized at least somewhat with the Central Powers. The great American Midwest was populated by large numbers of immigrants from German and Central European backgrounds.

Most Americans hated the idea of getting drawn into a European war. This isolationist view prevailed at first, although it became steadily more difficult for America to avoid playing a role in international affairs. As president, Woodrow Wilson faced a constant struggle between neutrality and isolationism on one hand and the economic and historic ties to Europe on the other.

"The example of America must be an example, not of peace because it will not fight, but of peace because peace is the healing and elevating influence of the world and strife is not," he said. "There is such a thing as a man being too proud to fight. There is such a thing as a man being so right that he does not need to convince others by force that he is right."

Wilson was shocked and deeply distressed by the grim brutality of "modern" warfare. Both sides dug lines of trenches along the border between Belgium and France, the Western Front, and suffered extreme losses during the slaughter that followed. The fighting raged on without either side winning a meaningful advantage. Appalling new weapons of mass destruction such as nerve gas and powerful explosives were used for the first time.

The last months of 1914 were desperate ones for the lonely president as he grappled both with his personal grief and with the great issues of a world at war. His daughters were grown, Jessie and Nell married, Margaret pursuing a musical career. The only woman in his household was his cousin, Helen Woodrow Bones, who had served as Ellen's personal secretary. "No one can offer Cousin Woodrow any word of comfort," she said, "for there is no comfort."

Wilson did try to fill the empty hours when he wasn't working. He played golf. He nurtured his growing friendship with his adviser, Edward House. He tried hard to follow Dr. Grayson's advice to stay busy and watch his health. But the months following Ellen Wilson's death were ones of despair.

The following spring, Wilson's worried friends and family introduced him to Edith Bolling Galt, an attractive and intelligent Washington widow. She had grown up in Virginia and had married the owner of a successful jewelry store in Washington. When her husband died, she had taken over the business herself and had run it so well that it had continued to prosper.

Edith Galt had a lively personality to go with her good looks. She had a sharp intelligence combined with a thoughtful, soft-spoken manner that made her appealing company to a man like

The president introduces his fiancée to an enthusiastic public at a baseball game. (The Library of Congress)

Edith Bolling Galt Wilson, Woodrow Wilson's second wife. (The Library of Congress)

Woodrow Wilson. This remarkable woman brought a lively gaiety to the gloomy White House during her increasingly frequent visits, providing exactly the right combination of feminine admiration and intellectual stimulation that Wilson craved.

To the delight of the matchmakers who had contrived to get the couple together, the stern and serious president fell in love, boyishly and lightheartedly so. He sought Edith Galt's company as often as he could, inviting her frequently to the White House. He took her for romantic drives in his presidential limousine, a big Pierce-Arrow convertible. He wrote her long letters. He had a special telephone line run between his room and her home. He sent her flowers every day. "The president was simply obsessed," said a White House staffer. "He put aside practically everything, dealing only with the most important matters of state."

Important matters of state continued to press. When a German submarine sank the *Lusitania*, a British ocean liner, there was a massive outcry in the United States. Public sentiment shifted away from neutrality and toward involvement in the war on the side of the Allies. The president faced enormous public pressure and increasingly complex issues. He felt desperately alone.

"I need you," he wrote to Edith. "I need you as a boy needs his sweetheart and a strong man his helpmate and heart's comrade." The *Lusitania* crisis deepened. The president faced ever more difficult decisions. His love and his need for Edith deepened, and he begged her to marry him. She reminded him that it had been less than a year since his wife's death. "In this place, time is not measured by weeks, or months, or years, but by deep human experiences," Woodrow replied. "Since her death, I have lived a lifetime of loneliness and heartache."

Eventually Edith accepted the president's proposal, and on December 18, 1915, Woodrow Wilson and Edith Bolling Galt were married in a quiet ceremony at her house in Washington. The next morning, as the newlyweds traveled to their honeymoon destination on a special train, an amused Secret Service agent watched the president emerge from his compartment dancing and singing a popular song. "Oh, you beautiful doll," Wilson crooned to his new wife, "you great big beautiful doll." It was a rare, light moment in trying times.

The uneasy neutrality grew ever harder to maintain. The British navy, strongest in the world, had blockaded Germany and stopped and seized cargoes bound for the Central Powers countries. Although the British paid for the seized cargoes, many Americans were enraged by such interference with U.S. shipping on the high seas. Such seizures were against international law and a violation of the neutral rights of the United States, the angry Americans claimed.

President Wilson sent strongly worded messages of protest to Great Britain, but the British claimed that they could not honor freedom of the seas when they were locked in a desperate fight for their survival. Wilson was urged by some to retaliate by banning exports to Britain, but the president, even though he was admittedly "about at the end of my patience with Great Britain and the Allies," refused such a drastic step. "The Allies are standing with their backs against the wall fighting wild beasts," he said.

Besides, there were even worse difficulties with Germany. Wilson had protested the sinking of the *Lusitania*, and Germany had promised that its submarines would not attack neutral ships or interfere with neutral shipping. In spite of the promise, Germany, desperate to break the British naval blockade of its ports, continued the submarine warfare. More than 200 American lives were lost.

When the Germans torpedoed the *Sussex*, a French steamer crossing the English Channel, and some Americans were among the eighty civilians killed, Wilson was outraged at tactics which disregarded "the fundamental rights of humanity." He warned Germany that if the attacks didn't stop right away, "the United States can have no choice but to sever diplomatic relations."

By the end of Wilson's first term of office, discussion of the war dominated conversations all over the nation. It was a major theme in the 1916 presidential election. Wilson was a reasonably popular president, but the public still perceived him as stiff and reserved. In order to challenge him, the Republicans nominated a man remarkably similar to Wilson, a scholarly, dignified Supreme Court justice named Charles Evans Hughes.

Wilson campaigned on the success of his New Freedom reforms and the fact that he had kept the nation out of war, in spite of his growing fears that neutrality was failing and war was likely. Hughes waged a decorous but vigorous campaign, charging that the New Freedom was ineffective and that Wilson's foreign policy was tentative and weak.

Everyone knew the election would be close. Wilson, calmly resigned to the possibility of defeat, had already decided that if Hughes won he would step aside so that the new president could take charge right away.

The election was so close that news of the outcome was painstakingly slow in coming. In the days before radio, late-breaking news was usually disseminated to the general public by special editions of newspapers, called extras. While Woodrow Wilson waited by a telephone to hear the results from Joe Tumulty, Americans all over the country waited for the extras to appear on the streets.

In a number of large cities, novel ways were devised to transmit the election results. *The New York Times* planned to flash a colored signal light from its building in Manhattan. In St. Louis, Missouri, the electric company would dim the lights in people's homes, one time for a Wilson victory, three times for Hughes.

As the votes were counted, it began to appear that Hughes had won. On election night a friend of Margaret Wilson called from New York to say that *The New York Times* had flashed a red light, the signal for a Hughes victory. The *New York World* put out a special bulletin declaring Hughes the winner. Just before midnight in St. Louis, the lights blinked once, tantalizingly, then twice more.

Americans all over the country, including Woodrow Wilson,

went to bed thinking the nation would have a new president.
Wilson calmly accepted his loss. Hughes believed he had won.
Then the vote from California, where Wilson had done surprisingly well with the progressives, tipped the balance back. The
next morning, Woodrow Wilson woke up to the happy news that
he had been reelected after all.

9

The War to End All Wars

After his reelection, President Wilson doubled his efforts to end the fighting in Europe and the growing specter of the direct involvement of the United States. Neither side had gained a clear advantage in the brutal fighting. The prospect of a decisive victory was dim for both sides, and the war was taking a fearsome toll. Europeans were tiring of the death, destruction, and despair. Woodrow Wilson hoped that the time was right to spearhead negotiations for a peaceful settlement.

During the month after the election, the president worked on a letter to the warring nations. He spent long hours over his typewriter as he juggled ideas, agonized over phrasing, and struggled to boil complex and divisive concepts into a compelling bid for peace, one that could motivate countries embroiled in a horrible war to put aside their differences and look for ways to end the conflict. The resulting letter was a clearly expressed and elegantly simple call for peace that asked each belligerent to spell out exactly what it was fighting for and what terms it would require for a suspension of hostilities.

When he sent the letter out a week before Christmas, Wilson had high hopes that the warring powers would discuss their differences and that a way to negotiate the end of the war might be found, but the letter failed to produce results. The Allies responded with a general list of their grievances and peace terms of total victory. The Germans and Central Powers refused even to state their requirements for peace.

The discouraged president decided to take his peace appeal directly to the people of the world in a ringing speech to the Senate in January of 1917. He called for "peace without victory" and declared that "only a peace between equals can last." He urged that an organization of nations be formed with the goal of preventing future wars. "No peace can last, or ought to last, which does not recognize and accept the principle that governments derive all their just powers from the consent of the governed and that no right anywhere exists to hand peoples about from sovereignty to sovereignty as if they were property."

But this noble definition of democracy also failed to produce any progress toward peace. In fact, it angered leaders of both the Allies and the Central Powers. The German government, which had temporarily suspended submarine warfare, announced an immediate resumption, prompting the United States to break off diplomatic relations.

More Americans were now calling for war, but President Wilson still wanted to wait. "I am less concerned with the attitude of the people than with what is right," he said at a stormy cabinet meeting.

As German acts of aggression continued, the voices calling for war grew louder and stronger. It became increasingly clear that the Germans were pushing for a quick victory before provoking the United States into war. American lives were lost in the torpedoing of British ships. Then came a series of direct attacks on American ships. Four were sunk.

The president realized that the United States's entry into the conflict could no longer be avoided. He agonized over his decision and delayed as long as he could, but on April 2, 1917, he went to Congress and asked for a formal declaration of war against Germany. Congress responded with resounding cheers, and on April 6 Woodrow Wilson signed the declaration that would plunge the United States fully into the "war to end all

President Wilson in his White House office. He often found the burden of wartime leadership heavy and put in long hours at his desk. (The Library of Congress)

wars," the war that was supposed to "make the world safe for democracy."

News of the war declaration against Germany flashed around the world. The American intervention came barely in time for the Allies, for whom defeat was dangerously close. The tide of trench warfare had turned against the French, who were dying by the thousands every day. The British were suffering heavy casualties. The Russian revolution had broken out, and the Bolsheviks were negotiating a separate peace with Germany, freeing German troops to leave the Eastern Front and fight against the remaining Allies, Britain and France, in the west.

President Wilson now faced the huge task of mobilizing America in time to turn the tide and save the Allied cause from defeat. Wilson knew that if American lives had to be sacrificed, fewer would be lost if the effort was massive and victory swift. To accomplish this would take extraordinary measures. It would be up to the president, who had fought so long to remain neutral, to lead the greatest military effort of all time.

Wilson's days were filled with decisions and tasks that came with relentless speed, each requiring action and leadership. He had hated the prospect of war and had struggled to avoid the necessity of it, but, now that it was here, he plunged into the job of winning it as quickly as possible. One historian noted ironically that Wilson has "attained far greater success in making war than in making peace."

The president now pushed his doubts aside, responding to the greatest American challenge with decisive leadership. He used his oratorical skill to unite Americans behind the cause. He used his ability to administer government efficiently to mobilize rapidly. He used his sharp intelligence to grasp tactical problems quickly and solve them promptly. Each day brought new crises. To handle the demand, the sixty-year-old president started early every morning and worked late into the night, pushing himself and the entire nation to new heights of effort.

At the beginning of the war, there were only about 200,000 soldiers in the United States Army. Twenty times that number would be needed for the fighting. The fairest way to raise the forces to the necessary level would be a draft, Wilson decided. Conscription was something that European refugees had come to America in droves to escape, so there was some strong objection to it, especially in the South and West, and some intense opposition in Congress. Wilson, however, having given the issue his usual thoughtful analysis, decided that conscription was necessary and pushed Congress hard to pass the Selective Service Act, the first nationwide military draft in U.S. history. The new law, passed on May 18, 1917, required all men between the ages of twenty-one and thirty to register for military service. Within weeks almost 10 million men had registered and more than 2 million had been drafted into the army. Before the war was over, American military strength would be up to more than 4 million.

The president's extraordinary ability to motivate Americans with brilliant oratory would be a vital factor in the mobilization for war and the
quest for peace. (The Library of Congress)

One of the president's greatest management skills was the ability to enlist the help of capable people, delegate authority to them, confer with them, then back them up once decisions had been made. Such a leadership style enabled him to concentrate on developing policy, making top-level decisions, and using his communication skills to generate vital public support for his programs. Wilson created special wartime agencies and boards and lined up top executives from the nation's greatest firms to run them. He found such superb military strategists as Gen. John Pershing to lead the armed forces and located skilled administrators to head government programs.

Once he had effective leadership in place, Wilson backed it up, standing firm against divisive pressure. Such pressure came from all kinds of sources. Former president Theodore Roosevelt, for example, leader of the famous Rough Riders in the Spanish-American War, approached him with the idea of getting together a special volunteer division that Roosevelt would personally lead against the Germans in France. Wilson gave him a firm no, enraging the popular Republican and some of his followers but giving General Pershing the freedom necessary to lead military operations without the interference of politicians.

The president did remain open to new ideas, though. When a young army captain approached him about raising a division of National Guard units from each state, Wilson saw potential for leadership in the young officer, promoted him to colonel, and sent him to serve under General Pershing. The name of the innovative soldier was George Patton.

Wilson also turned aside an attempt by Congress to meddle with military strategy. He took a great deal of heat from political opponents and some segments of the public for his unwavering stand, but the overall result was a high degree of leadership effectiveness and public confidence in his ability to conduct the war.

Even the Allies presented problems for the president. The new soldiers and their equipment had to be transported to

Europe, along with food and supplies for the desperate Allies. The route to the continent was across the Atlantic, infested with deadly German U-boats, or submarines. To cross the ocean safely, Wilson and his advisers decided that a system of convoys was the best method. The proud British navy, used to unrivaled domination of the seas, balked at being told what to do by the Americans, forcing the exasperated president to push hard for the convoy concept. Fortunately, this system, in which troopships and supply ships sailed in a group surrounded by an escort of destroyers, worked out well, and not a single American troopship was sunk.

The president also exerted his leadership to rally the people behind the war effort. Americans cooperated by observing meatless days, wheatless days, sweetless days, and heatless days to conserve vital food and fuel. When men were drafted, women worked in the nation's factories, keeping wartime production up. Students from exclusive women's colleges spent summers operating farm machinery in order to keep food production steady.

Believing in leadership by example, the president and his family got the White House into the effort. When it was necessary for the nation to observe gasless Sundays to save gasoline, President and Mrs. Wilson went to church in a horse-drawn carriage escorted by policemen on bicycles. Vegetable gardens were planted on the White House grounds, and a flock of sheep was even brought in to graze on the White House lawns. When the sheep were later sheared, the wool was auctioned off at a hefty profit to benefit the American Red Cross.

War on such a massive scale brought all kinds of sweeping social change. To pay for the estimated $35 billion it would cost, Wilson pushed Congress to establish an income tax and special taxes on the wartime profits of American companies. These and other new taxes didn't raise enough money, though, making it necessary to borrow the difference. Instead of borrowing heavily from private banks, Wilson decided to rely on the sale of bonds directly to the public and persuaded Americans to invest as much as they could in the new Liberty Bonds.

The changing role of women in American wartime society accelerated their demands for suffrage, the right to vote. Wilson, who had been previously indifferent to the political rights of women, now gave them his support and appeared before the Senate to ask for approval of the Nineteenth Amendment to the Constitution, guaranteeing women the right to vote. "Our safety in these questioning days will depend upon the direct and authoritative participation of women in our counsels," he said.

Less desirable social and political changes came too. There was an increase in bigotry, intolerance, and antiimmigrant feeling. Some precious American civil liberties were suspended. Censorship was imposed, and laws were passed making it a crime to criticize the government, the flag, or even army uniforms. The Committee on Public Information was established to help generate public support for the war effort. An unfortunate side effect was a flood of blatant propaganda, giving weight to the adage that "truth is the first casualty of war." School textbooks were rewritten to portray Americans as shining idealists and Germans as depraved Huns. Sauerkraut was given a new name, Liberty cabbage, and dachshunds were called Liberty pups. The use of German books and the teaching of the German language were banned in schools. A fever of hatred was directed at anything German, leading to dangerous vigilantism and excessive persecution of innocent citizens in the name of freedom.

Wilson had foreseen these excesses. He had told a friend that if Americans were led into war, they would forget there ever was such a thing as tolerance." Even so, he did little to temper the exercise of dangerous wartime powers given to the censors, propagandists, and protectors. He believed that legislation such as the Espionage Act and the Trading-with-the-Enemy Act clearly showed that Congress was determined to suppress anything that might undermine the war effort and that some members of Congress were among the most enthusiastic of the

Posters such as this one were used to motivate Americans to support the war effort. (The Library of Congress)

zealots. Suppression of dissent was, he believed, a necessary price for national unity.

The great buildup of American armed forces, public support, and citizen effort accomplished what it had to. The first American soldiers landed in France in June of 1917. By the next summer, American ranks had swelled to 300,000, with the total rising to more than 2 million before the fighting finally ended. Although they had been quickly trained and rushed into battle, the American doughboys learned quickly and soon earned the respect of the battle-weary Allied troops. Before the arrival of the Americans, the Allies were on the brink of defeat. Gradually the American effort turned the tide.

10

Battling for Peace

Even before America's entrance into the war, Woodrow Wilson was grappling with the issues of peace, analyzing the situation from his careful scholar's perspective, and formulating plans that he believed would enhance the chances for long-range peace. Although he was an advocate of neutrality in the period before World War I, he wasn't strictly an isolationist, because he believed America did have an important international role to play, that of peacemaker.

Wilson's dream was to fashion a policy that would foster the prospects for peace, and he passionately believed that the nation he led should exert strong moral influence in this area. If the bloody slaughter of this violent war was to be worth the great sacrifices it had required, it would be in providing an opportunity to prevent future wars.

So while the American Expeditionary Forces battled beside the Allies, and American soldiers fell by the thousands in the brutal fighting, Wilson worked on his plans for peace. The key to lasting peace, he knew, would lie in the conditions of surrender and the terms of any treaties at the end of the war. To avoid containing the seeds of the next war, the peace would have to be fair to the losers as well as to the winners. If the suffering of the losers was too great, resentments would start to simmer, eventually boiling over into new conflict.

Wilson's goal was "peace without victory" and surrender without revenge. That would mean convincing the Allies to agree to generosity instead of vengeance. To achieve such a peace would require brilliant statesmanship, delicate negotiations, and extraordinary diplomacy.

Wilson proposed his peace plan to the world ten months before the war ended. In a historic speech before Congress on January 8, 1918, he outlined his ideas in the form of a series of fourteen points. The Fourteen Points offered the framework upon which a just and lasting peace could be built. In a combination of general philosophical goals and specific objectives, the points provided guidelines for the negotiating process, particulars for the realignment of European borders and colonial empires after the war, and a way to work out future disputes without war.

The first point called for an open peace negotiation process, condemning secret talks and side deals between parties. The second called for freedom of the seas, the third for removal of barriers to open trade by ending or equalizing tariffs, and the fourth for orderly disarmament. The fifth point called for an end to colonialism and the opportunity for people under colonial rule to participate in governing themselves.

The sixth point tried to guarantee that the Russian people, in the process of revolt, would have the opportunity to choose their own destiny by requiring the withdrawal of all foreign troops from Russia. The next series of points, seven through thirteen, dealt with similar guarantees to the peoples of Europe by outlining a just realignment of borders and the evacuation of all foreign troops.

The fourteenth point was, to Wilson, the most important. It called for the formation of a peacekeeping organization of nations. "A general association of nations must be formed under specific covenants for the purpose of affording mutual guarantees of political independence and territorial integrity to great and small states alike."

Wilson hoped that if he announced his peace plan in advance, the Germans, facing probable defeat, might be inclined to negotiate an early end to the carnage, realizing that there would be no unfair revenge and unjust reprisals. "We wish her only to accept a place of equality among the peoples of the world . . . instead of a place of mastery," he said of Germany.

Once he had made the Fourteen Points public, Wilson embarked on a delicate course of negotiation, persuasion, and coercion that he hoped and prayed would lead to their implementation. The Allies, scenting victory and hoping to extract reparations and retribution from Germany, were not at all interested in Wilson's plan until Wilson sent Colonel House to Paris to apply the strongest possible pressure. The Germans still hoped to regain the military advantage. They had developed new weapons of war such as airplanes equipped with explosive devices called bombs and poison gas. There might, they believed, still be a chance of German victory.

The influx of fresh American troops, though, had had an electrifying effect, enough to revitalize the war-weary Allied forces, who gained steady ground against Germany. While the fighting raged in the forests of France and in the trenches along the Western Front, Wilson reminded the leaders of France, Britain, and Italy that America was not a member of the alliance but rather an associated power. If the Allies didn't accept the Fourteen Points, the United States would negotiate with Germany on its own. The threat worked, and the Allies grudgingly agreed to accept all but one of the points. Britain refused to give on the issue of freedom of the seas.

The last convincing German offensive was turned back in bitter fighting at the Marne River in July of 1918. By August, the German stronghold at Amiens had been wiped out. In September, the Americans joined French troops in an attack on a key German position on the Meuse River, scoring a decisive victory in two days of bloody combat that claimed more than 7,000 casualties. In October, more than a million Americans battled through the Argonne Forest near the border of Belgium, dealing Germany another massive defeat.

Germany sent a message to Wilson saying it was ready to sign an armistice based on the Fourteen Points. Wilson replied that he would negotiate only with a government that represented the German people, not the German military leaders. He insisted that the kaiser step aside and a new government be put in place. After some further wrangling with the still-reluctant Allies, who wanted to invade Germany and conquer it completely, the warring nations finally agreed on terms. An armistice was signed on the eleventh hour of the eleventh day of the eleventh month, November 11, 1918.

"The armistice was signed this morning," President Wilson announced to his fellow Americans. "Everything for which America fought has been accomplished. It will now be our fortunate duty to assist by example, by sober, friendly counsel and by material aid in the establishment of just democracy throughout the world." When the slaughter finally ended, the Great War had claimed the lives of more than 10 million people.

Once the armistice had been signed, plans were made for a peace conference where the details of a permanent treaty would be worked out. Wilson's passionate dream was to get his Fourteen Points accepted by the other participants in the Paris conference, resulting in a just peace and the formation of a League of Nations to enforce it. In his pursuit of peace, though, Wilson made a series of unfortunate mistakes, mistakes that would eventually deprive him of the victory he so fiercely desired.

In the congressional elections of 1918, he had made peace a partisan issue by urging voters to elect Democrats as a show of support for the Fourteen Points. "I earnestly beg that you will express yourself unmistakably to that effect by returning a Democratic majority to both the Senate and the House," he said. "The leaders of the minority of the present congress have unquestionably been pro war, but they have been anti-administration. At almost every turn since we entered the war they have sought to take the choice of policy and the conduct of the war out of my hands and put in under the control of instrumentalities of their own choosing," he continued in his stinging partisan attack. "The return of a Republican majority would certainly be interpreted on the other side of the water as a repudiation of my leadership."

Edith Wilson became an active partner to her husband and assisted him extensively. (The Library of Congress)

Republicans, many of whom had put their party loyalty second to their loyalty to their country and supported Wilson throughout the war, were incensed. Voters responded to the resulting outcry by giving the Republicans a small majority in both the House of Representatives and the Senate.

Wilson compounded this mistake by failing to name any Republican senators to the peace conference delegation. Because the Constitution requires that the Senate approve any treaties into which the United States might enter, the support of the Republicans would eventually be required. Including one or two influential Republican senators on the negotiating team would have been a good way to generate such support. Wilson was repeatedly urged to do so, but he stubbornly resisted.

Instead, Wilson unwisely named men such as Secretary of State Robert Lansing, who had replaced the pacifist William Jennings Bryan, and his adviser Edward House. House was known to have strong pro-British sentiments, making him less willing to push for freedom of the seas and other points to which the British objected. Lansing's enthusiasm for the Fourteen Points was lukewarm at best. Worse, Lansing had already expressed reservations about the League of Nations, the most important of all the Fourteen Points to Wilson. ✕

Wilson made his biggest mistake of all, many historians say, by trying to lead the Paris delegation himself. He sincerely believed that he alone had a clear vision of the peace that was possible. He thought that the other Allied nations, unless held tightly in check at the negotiating table, would seek vengeful terms. He was genuinely afraid to entrust such sacred and delicate diplomacy to anyone else. "It is now my duty to play my full part in making good what they . . . offered their life's blood to obtain. I can think of no call to service which could transcend this," he said in announcing his decision to attend the talks.

Although he may have been right, the president didn't really need to attend the conference in person. He could have sent a representative to coordinate the diplomatic efforts on his behalf. Another negotiator would probably have been less passionate and better able to compromise in the labyrinth of delicate maneuvering that lay ahead. Wilson was a strong leader, but he wasn't a particularly skillful diplomat. He would have been better off to remain behind and exert his influence from a distance. Such a strategy would have allowed him to stand firm on the important main themes without becoming mired in all the necessary, but distracting, detail.

There were other good reasons for him not to go. He was badly needed at home to shepherd the nation through the critical postwar period. His leadership would be essential to restore the peacetime economy and revive the New Freedom. His influence and persuasive skill could help prepare the Senate and the American people to accept a peace treaty based on the Fourteen Points. And, very important, forgoing the long and stressful trip would protect the president's already fragile health. Once he decided to go to Paris, however, Wilson obstinately refused to listen to all those who advised against it, taking such advice as a personal affront.

Of course, Wilson hadn't foreseen all these problems. He didn't fully realize that Americans were not united about the terms of peace as they had been about winning the war. He didn't understand how much they wanted to forget the war and get on with their lives. And he underestimated the depth of their hatred for the Germans.

But Wilson wasn't aware of just how badly he had sabotaged himself, so he left for Paris with buoyant expectations and high spirits. The wildly enthusiastic welcome he received in Europe bolstered his optimism and reinforced his stubborn confidence. From the moment his ship, the *George Washington*, reached the French port of Brest, cheering multitudes of grateful Europeans greeted the American president as their savior. "Vive Wilson!" they shouted in roaring adulation. "Long live Wilson!"

The jubilance of the people wasn't shared by their leaders, though. Delegates from thirty-six countries who had officially been at war with the Central Powers attended the peace conference, but four men, Wilson, Premier Georges Clemenceau of France, Prime Minister David Lloyd George of Great Britain, and Prime Minister Vittorio Orlando of Italy, were expected to dominate the talks.

The peace conference involved not only the official delegates from each of the participating countries, but aides, advisers, and clerks numbering in the thousands. There were more than 1,300 people in the contingent from the United States. When Wilson reached Paris, a round of parties, receptions, and ceremonies immediately started. Wilson wanted to get going on the peace talks right away, but there were delays. The other Big Four leaders suggested that the American president tour the

President Wilson at the peace conference in France in 1919. (The
Library of Congress)

rest of Europe while the conference preliminaries were taking
place.

Some historians believe that the delay and subsequent sug-
gestion for Wilson's triumphal tour were a cynical appeal to his
ego to get him out of the way for a while. Others think that the
Allies wanted Wilson to experience the genuine outpouring of
gratitude for the Americans. Probably their motive was a little
of both, but, whatever the reason, Wilson traveled to England
and Italy to receive the overwhelming accolades of the people.

The welcome Wilson received from the wildly cheering mobs
in England was even greater, if such a thing were possible, than
the adulation of the people of France. As his procession passed
through the streets of London, the flowers tossed by school-
girls became a shower of color. The blossoms piled up around

Woodrow and Edith. They were buried almost to their waists as they waved to the frantic crowds. How ironic, Wilson thought, that his childhood heroes had been British statesmen and now the British were hailing an American statesman as their hero.

In Italy, the cheering was even more thunderous. The greatest crowds in Italian history jammed the streets of Rome to cry, shout, and practically worship the American president. Wilson was moved by the almost godlike treatment, but it concerned him too. "I am now at the apex of my glory in the hearts of these people," he said. "I have got to pool the interests of Italy with the interests of the world. When I do that, I am afraid they are going to be disappointed and turn about and hiss me."

The peace conference finally got going in January 1919. The other leaders of the Big Four thought Wilson's lofty plan and noble sentiments were impractical. The American president seemed unrealistic and naive to the seasoned and savvy Europeans. "Wilson with his Fourteen Points is worse than God almighty, who only had ten!" sneered the cynical French premier as he began to realize that the American president actually meant what he said in his high-toned speeches. "He thinks he is the first man in two thousand years to know anything about peace on earth."

The Allied negotiators battled Wilson on almost every point. The others all wanted the treaty to have a "War Guilt" clause, an admission by Germany of full responsibility for starting the war and an agreement to pay for it. France and Britain wanted Germany to pay more than $120 billion in reparations. Many countries wanted to annex German territory or take over former German colonies. Some demanded harsh punishment for German citizens. Most of them wanted to put off a commitment to the League of Nations, pressuring Wilson to agree to a basic peace treaty first and work on organizing the league later.

Although he was eventually forced to compromise on other issues, the American president insisted that a League of Nations charter be the first section of the treaty. To achieve his goal, Wilson drove himself and his staff past the point of exhaustion, working from dawn to midnight day after day. He attended meetings, made speeches, drafted a covenant for the League of Nations, labored over endless documents, followed up on thousands of details. The American contingent was, observed one correspondent, "the hardest-driven commission in Paris."

Edith Wilson and Dr. Grayson worried about the president's declining health, but Wilson refused to spare himself, growing more gaunt and gray as the difficult negotiations ground on. The fight took all his powers of persuasion and every ounce of moral force he could muster. He dipped deep into the last reserves of his strength. At one point he threatened to leave the conference and deal directly with Germany. He might give some on other issues, but he absolutely refused to compromise on the League of Nations. Finally, after weeks of wrangling, Woodrow Wilson's proudest moment came when he presented the League of Nations covenant for unanimous adoption by the peace conference on February 14, 1919.

He stood before the other conference delegates, who jammed the room, but he spoke to the citizens of the world. "A living thing is born," he said after reading the covenant, which he characterized as practical and humane. "There is a pulse of sympathy in it. There is a compulsion of conscience throughout it. It is practical, and yet it is intended to purify, to rectify, to elevate."

11

The Vision Fades

The League of Nations covenant was adopted as the first section of the permanent peace treaty, but the conference had much more work to do. Next came the thorny matters of border alignments, refugee resettlement, reparations, colonial empires, tariffs, and trade. Woodrow Wilson decided to return briefly to the United States while the preliminary discussions on these issues were taking place. The president had been in Europe for more than two months, and there were urgent matters for him to take care of at home. The final session of Congress was due to adjourn, and the president needed to study all the bills that had been passed and decide whether to sign each one into law or veto it. He also wanted to lobby senators for support on the League of Nations and to communicate with the American people about its importance.

Wilson's ship landed in Boston, where the governor of Massachusetts, Calvin Coolidge, was waiting, along with thousands of wildly cheering ordinary Americans, to greet him. "We welcome him as the representative of a great people, as a great statesman, as one whom we assure we will support in the future in working out of that destiny," Coolidge said.

But the governor's encouraging words did not reflect the feelings of many senators. There was trouble brewing, trouble that Wilson tried to deflect by inviting members of the Senate Foreign Relations Committee and other influential legislators to dinner at the White House. The chairman of the Senate Foreign Relations Committee was Henry Cabot Lodge, a longtime adversary of the president. He attended the dinner, but he sat silently, grim and intractable. Other lawmakers were less overtly hostile, but they asked lots of tough questions, expressed numerous doubts, and insisted on changes in the treaty.

Wilson was furious with the senators, particularly Lodge. "The first thing I am going to tell the people on the other side of the water is that an overwhelming majority of the American people is in favor of the League of Nations," he snapped in a vitriolic speech in New York the night before he sailed back to France. "I am amazed—not alarmed but amazed—that there should be in some quarters such a comprehensive ignorance of the state of the world!"

Bitter and stubborn, Wilson returned to the peace conference, where more discouragement awaited him. While he was gone, the American delegation had been pressured by the French and British to make unacceptable concessions. Grim, determined, and exhausted, Wilson settled again into the grueling negotiations, which were to continue for three more long months.

As the talks, meetings, discussions, and work continued, people began to notice changes in Wilson. His temper grew shorter. He seemed restless and petulant. A chronic tic developed in his cheek, causing an obvious distortion of the left side of his face. In early April he developed a high fever, violent cough, and diarrhea. He was so sick that Dr. Grayson wondered if he had been poisoned.

Dr. Grayson stayed with his gravely ill patient through the night of April 3, as Wilson's fever climbed to 103 degrees. He feared that the president could be dying. By morning, though, Wilson was a little better. The doctor diagnosed influenza but told the press that the president had a cold.

Although it's not possible to say for sure, modern medical experts think it likely that Wilson suffered a stroke that night. Many of his symptoms, particularly the small changes in his personality, were characteristic of a minor cerebral thrombosis.

Whatever caused the illness, it sapped the strength of the already frail president. Even so, Wilson battled back, making an amazing recovery. He insisted on directing the treaty negotiations and stubbornly held out for his way on major issues.

Of course he had to compromise, but he pushed the French and British to compromise as well. Eventually the complex treaty took shape, with the League of Nations covenant fundamentally intact within it. Although there were serious deviations from the Fourteen Points and other potential problems, Wilson reasoned that the League of Nations would be able to oversee the arbitration of any resulting disputes and could be appealed to to mitigate the harsher terms. By late June the treaty was complete and signed by Germany and the Allies. Woodrow Wilson once again headed home.

Now he had to convince two-thirds of the Senate to ratify the treaty, which committed the United States to membership in the new League of Nations. On July 10, 1919, President Wilson presented the results of his work to the Senate. "The League of Nations was not merely an instrument to adjust and remedy old wrongs under a new treaty of peace; it was the only hope for mankind," Wilson told the senators. "Shall we or any other free people hesitate to accept this great duty? Dare we reject it and break the heart of the world?"

Rejection by the Senate, though, was a distinct possibility. Most senators were willing to support the treaty if some modifications were made, but Wilson steadfastly refused to agree to any compromise. The opposition, led by Senator Lodge, was angered by Wilson's unyielding stance, and resistance hardened on both sides.

Wilson then decided to appeal directly to the people and planned to embark on a speaking tour across the nation. He had supreme confidence in his ability to convince the American people of the essential rightness of the League of Nations. Once he had reached the people, he believed, they would exert a moral pressure that the Senate would not dare resist.

His wife and his doctor tried to talk him out of going. He was

The president recalled his visit to an American cemetery in France during his last great public speech, an appeal to the public to support ratification of the treaty establishing the League of Nations (Pueblo, Colorado, September 25, 1919). (The Library of Congress)

a sick man and the strain could kill him, they warned. But Wilson was determined. The League of Nations, he insisted, was worth any price he might have to pay. Nothing, not even his life, was more important than peace. "You must remember that I, as commander in chief, was responsible for sending our soldiers to Europe. In the crucial test in the trenches they did not turn back," he told Dr. Grayson. "I cannot turn back now. I cannot put my personal safety, my health in the balance against my duty. I must go."

In early September, Woodrow and Edith Wilson, along with Dr. Grayson, Joseph Tumulty, a group of reporters, several secretaries, and the usual contingent of Secret Service agents, boarded a special train. In a grueling, whirlwind twenty-two days, the president made thirty-four impassioned speeches. He warned over and over again that without the League of Nations "within another generation there will be another world war."

The next war, he said, would be even more destructive. "What the Germans used were toys compared to what would be used in the next war," he warned. That war would be "another struggle in which not a few hundred thousand fine men from America will have to die, but as many millions."

Although he suffered from blinding headaches, acute indigestion, and intense fatigue, the president persevered. He seemed driven, as indeed he was. The fight for the League of Nations had become a mission to him. At times he seemed too frail and sick to speak. Often he appeared to be near collapse, but the warm reception of the audience always seemed to give him enough strength to go on.

On September 25, Wilson made an especially inspired address in Pueblo, Colorado. "Again and again, my fellow citizens, mothers who lost their sons in France have come to me and, taking my hand, have shed tears upon it not only, but they have added, 'God bless you, Mr. President!' Why, my fellow citizens, should they pray God to bless me? I advised the Congress of the United States to create the situation that led to the death of their sons. I ordered their sons overseas. I consented to their sons being put in the most difficult parts of the battle line, where death was certain, as in the impenetrable difficulties of the forest of Argonne. Why should they weep upon my hand and call down the blessings of God upon me? Because they believe that their boys died for something that vastly transcends any of the immediate and palpable objects of the war. They believe, and they rightly believe, that their sons saved the liberty of the world. They believe that wrapped up with the liberty of the world is the continuous protection of that liberty by the concerted powers of all civilized people. They believe that this sacrifice was made in order that other sons should not be called upon for a similar gift, the gift of life, the gift of all that died."

The president described a visit he had made to a cemetery in France where American soldiers lay buried. "I wish some men in public life who are now opposing the settlement for which these men died could visit such a spot as that. I wish the thought that comes out of those graves could penetrate their consciousness. I wish that they could feel the moral obligation that rests upon us not to go back on those boys, but to see the thing through, to see it through to the end and make good their redemption of the world. For nothing less depends upon this decision, nothing less than the liberation and salvation of the world."

In an inspiring conclusion, Wilson urged all America to take up the fight for peace. "There is one thing that the American people always rise to and extend their hand to, and that is the truth of justice and of liberty and of peace. We have accepted that truth and we are going to be led by it, and it is going to lead us, and through us the world, out into the pastures of quietness and peace such as the world never dreamed of before."

The crowd roared with applause, and Wilson left the speaker's platform with good reason to hope that the old oratorical magic was working and that the people were responding to his fundamental cry for what was right and just. Although he was completely drained physically, he boarded the train in a positive frame of mind. The next stop was Wichita.

As the train rumbled across the Great Plains, the president's intense headache grew even worse, causing him to suffer an explosion of pain that left him trembling and weak. Dr. Grayson stopped the train and took the president out for a short walk in the cool evening air. That seemed to help a little, but Wilson was obviously too sick to continue the tour.

Edith Wilson and Dr. Grayson were able to persuade the president to return to Washington for some desperately needed rest only by reminding him that he looked so ill that he could harm, rather than help, the cause of peace if he continued. Finally Wilson agreed to go back to Washington, and the train sped home. A week later he suffered a massive stroke and collapsed, his left side paralyzed.

While Wilson hovered at the brink of death for several weeks his wife, for all practical purposes, functioned as the president of the United States. She and the doctor kept all news of the president's grave condition from the press and the public. When, against all odds, Wilson began to recover, Edith Wilson shielded him from as much pressure as she could. It was the president's wife, therefore, who determined who would see him and what matters would be brought to his attention. And it was the president's wife who had the ability to influence his decisions.

By the time the Senate was ready to vote on the peace treaty, on November 19, Wilson's mind was clear and he was able to sit up in bed. Edith Wilson allowed a visit from a sympathetic senator, who came to tell the president that unless he would allow some of Lodge's reservations, the treaty would not pass. The senator suggested compromise.

"Let Lodge compromise!" Wilson snapped.

The Senate voted twice, first on Lodge's reservations, which were defeated, then on the treaty without the Lodge reservations, which was also defeated. In March 1920 there was one last effort. The treaty was introduced again. Wilson was again urged to compromise, and again he refused. Again, the treaty was defeated, this time for good.

12

A Place in History

Although Woodrow Wilson made a limited recovery from his stroke, he was never again well enough to function fully as the nation's president. For his last year and a half in office, he was an invalid shielded by his wife and his doctor, an unprecedented situation that the Constitution did not directly provide for. The Constitution said that the vice president should take over if the president was not able to "discharge the powers and duties" of the office, but it did not spell out the circumstances under which the president would be unable to perform such duties or who would make such a decision.

The secretary of state approached Edith Wilson to suggest that the president resign and be replaced by the vice president, but that advice was abruptly rejected and Woodrow Wilson served out his full term. Some historians say that he was president in name only and that Edith Wilson virtually ran the country. Others believe that, although weak, he retained his mental faculties and made important decisions.

Rumors of the president's disability swirled around the capital, prompting Congress to investigate by sending Senator Albert Fall to see Wilson in person. If the senator found the president to be seriously impaired, leaders of the Senate would consider starting impeachment proceedings in order to resolve the crisis of leadership.

When Senator Fall arrived, though, Wilson was having one of his better days. He was propped up with his paralyzed arm covered by a shawl. He greeted Fall with a firm handshake. The

Some of Woodrow Wilson's critics saw him as prim, pompous, and unyielding, as he is portrayed in this caricature. (The Library of Congress)

Edith Wilson is thought by some historians to have functioned as an acting president during her husband's illness. (The Library of Congress)

two men held a short talk during which the president made lucid comments on a number of issues. He even managed to resurrect his famous wit when Senator Fall, an old adversary, got up to leave.

"Mr. President," the senator said, "I am praying for you."

"Which way, Senator?" the president asked with a wry smile.

Senator Fall reported to his congressional colleagues that the president seemed alert, and the idea of impeachment was abandoned.

During his last months in office, the president was unable to attend to any but the most important of matters, those brought to his attention by his wife. After the war he had spent six months in Paris and then had devoted his remaining time and energy to pushing for the League of Nations, which still ob-

Two of the former president's granddaughters listen as Wilson speaks for the first time on radio, giving an Armistice Day address in 1923. (The Library of Congress)

sessed him to the exclusion of almost everything else. The result was an unfortunate lack of domestic leadership right after the war, a critical period characterized by labor problems, social unrest, and growing racial tensions.

Although he was still a great hero to much of the world, most Americans had lost confidence in Wilson. The Democratic party nominated the governor of Ohio, James M. Cox, as its candidate for the presidency in 1920, but the election was overwhelmingly won by the Republican nominee, Warren G. Harding, who capitalized on voters' postwar concerns and campaigned on the theme of a "return to normalcy."

Wilson remained an invalid for his last months in the White House, a discouraged and sometimes bitter man. One bright note was the announcement in December that he had been awarded the prestigious Nobel Peace Prize. In March of 1921, his term was over. He rode to the Capitol with Warren Harding on Inauguration Day, signed a few last-minute bills and documents, met briefly with a few members of Congress, and left quietly as his successor was being sworn in, too weak and racked with pain to go outside and stand beside the new president.

Edith and Woodrow Wilson moved to a comfortable house in a residential Washington neighborhood, where the former president quietly lived out his final three years. The last time he spoke to the American people was in a special radio address in November 1923. It was the first time he had spoken over this new communication medium. "The only way in which we can worthily give proof of our appreciation of the high significance of Armistice Day," he said, "is to put self-interest away and once more formulate and act upon the highest ideals."

The next morning, a reverent crowd, once again inspired by the powerful words of Woodrow Wilson, gathered in front of his house. On the day marking the end of the World War, the end that he had struggled so hard to negotiate, Wilson emerged to speak briefly. He was greeted with warm applause. "I have seen fools resist Providence before, and I have seen their destruction," he said. "That we shall prevail is as sure as that God reigns." The applause swelled to one last crescendo. "Thank you," the former president said before going back inside. Six weeks later, on February 3, 1924, he quietly died at the age of sixty-seven.

As president, Woodrow Wilson led the nation through the early crises of the twentieth century. Today, as that century draws to a close, his presidency is viewed as a pivotal period in American history, a time when the United States emerged as a major world power and the old order started to change.

Wilson's prophecy of war within a generation would prove heartbreakingly true. Although the League of Nations was formed in January of 1920, it operated without the United States, which never did join. For a few years it served as an arbitrator of territorial disputes, but it was unable to prevent the nations of Europe from forming new military alliances, which eventually resulted in the outbreak of World War II.

In the failure of the League of Nations, though, were the seeds of success for a new organization that was formed in 1946, after the Second World War. The United Nations eventually fulfilled Wilson's dream of an international organization dedicated to

Woodrow and Edith Wilson moved to this house on S Street in Washington after his presidency was over. He died here on February 3, 1924. (The Library of Congress)

peace. Some historians say that Wilson was ahead of his time—that the lost peace and another war were necessary to make the United Nations possible, that there were some lessons the people of the world simply had to learn the hard way. Certainly the steady progress toward real world peace that is now being made by the United Nations is a lasting tribute to the vision of Woodrow Wilson.

Was Woodrow Wilson perfect? Obviously not. Was he great? Perhaps. Was he sincere and idealistic? Definitely. Did he make a difference in his world? Without question. The human qualities of Woodrow Wilson contributed to both his stunning success and his greatest failures. He was an intensely human mixture of the good and the not so good.

"He was sincere in his principles, and he had the courage to stand for them in the face of all consequences," said his physician and friend Dr. Cary Grayson. "He broke with some of his friends, and the breaks hurt him, but these severances were due to differences on some matter of principle."

"Spiritually he dwelt beyond the snowline," said British Prime Minister Lloyd George, "in an atmosphere pure, glistening, and bracing—but cold."

"You could work for, but not always with, Wilson," commented one of the young preceptors Woodrow Wilson had brought to Princeton. "He was dominant always, or he was restless and dissatisfied."

"Intuition rather than reason played the chief part in the way in which he reached conclusions and judgments," said Robert Lansing, who served as secretary of state. "In fact arguments, however soundly reasoned, did not appeal to him if they were opposed to his feeling of what was the right thing to do."

"He struggled to introduce ethical considerations into the conduct of world affairs," wrote Bernard Baruch, one of Wilson's political advisers. "Confronted by a choice between the right as he saw it and the expedient, he invariably chose the right."

"In my opinion his one chief fault was his failure to recognize the relativity of right and truth. These were absolutes with him and therefore he could not compromise with other standards and opinions," said a Princeton professor.

"He was a titanic failure," wrote historian Gerald W. Johnson. But "a failure gigantic enough leaves upon the world an impression far more lasting than an ordinary success."

This huge painting, supposedly the largest of Woodrow Wilson in the world, was exhibited on the steps of the United States Treasury Building in Washington. (The Library of Congress)

Woodrow Wilson himself probably gave the best analysis of his own performance. "I feel tonight like a man who is lodging happily in the inn which lies half way along the journey," he said early in his presidency. "We shall go the rest of the journey and sleep at the journey's end like men with a quiet conscience, knowing that we have served our fellow men and have, thereby, tried to serve God."

Woodrow Wilson knew that he would have to wait and let history be his judge. "I have a sincere desire to serve, to be of some little assistance in improving the condition of the average man," he once wrote. "In doing this, I try hard to purge my heart of selfish motives. It will only be known when I am dead whether or not I have succeeded."

Index